THE BLUE FLOWER

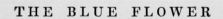

In the City of Saloma.

THE BLUE FLOWER

BY
HENRY VAN DYKE

The desire of the moth for the star,
Of the night for the morrow,
The devotion to something afar
From the sphere of our sorrow.
—SHELLEY

ILLUSTRATED

NEW YORK
CHARLES SCRIBNER'S SONS
MDCCCCVI

*Printed, October, 1902. Reprint-
ed, December, 1902; March, October, 1903; April, October, 1904
July, 1905. November, 1906*

PREFACE

SOMETIMES short stories are brought together like parcels in a basket. Sometimes they grow together like blossoms on a bush. Then, of course, they really belong to one another, because they have the same life in them.

The stories in this book have been growing together for a long time. It is at least ten years since the first of them, the story of *The Other Wise Man*, came to me; and all the others I knew quite well by heart a good while before I could find the time, in a hard-worked life, to write them down and try to make them clear and true to others. It has been a slow task, because the right word has not always been easy to find, and I wanted to keep free from conventionality in the thought and close to nature in the picture. It is enough to cause a man no little shame to see how small is the fruit of so long labour.

And yet, after all, when one wishes to write

about life, especially about that part of it which is inward, the inwrought experience of living may be of value. And that is a thing which one cannot get in haste, neither can it be made to order. Patient waiting belongs to it; and rainy days belong to it; and the best of it sometimes comes in the doing of tasks that seem not to amount to much. So in the long run, I suppose, while delay and failure and interruption may keep a piece of work very small, yet in the end they enter into the quality of it and bring it a little nearer to the real thing, which is always more or less of a secret.

But the strangest part of it all is the way in which a single thought, an idea, will live with a man while he works, and take new forms from year to year, and light up the things that he sees and hears, and lead his imagination by the hand into many wonderful and diverse regions. It seems to me that there are two ways in which you may give unity to a book of stories. You may stay in one place and write about different themes, preserving always the colour of the same locality. Or you may go into different places and use as many of the colours and shapes of life as you can really see in the light of the same thought.

There is such a thought in this book. It is the idea of the search for inward happiness, which all men who are really alive are following, along what various paths, and with what different fortunes! Glimpses of this idea, traces of this search, I thought that I could see in certain tales that were in my mind,—tales of times old and new, of lands near and far away. So I tried to tell them, as best as I could, hoping that other men, being also seekers, might find some meaning in them.

There are only little, broken chapters from the long story of life. None of them is taken from other books. Only one of them—the story of Winifried and the Thunder-Oak—has the slightest wisp of a foundation in fact or legend. Yet I think they are all true.

But how to find a name for such a book,—a

PREFACE

name that will tell enough to show the thought and yet not too much to leave it free? I have borrowed a symbol from the old German poet and philosopher, *Novalis,* to stand instead of a name. The Blue Flower which he used in his romance of *Heinrich von Ofterdingen* to symbolise Poetry, the object of his young hero's quest, I have used here to signify happiness, the satisfaction of the heart.

Reader, will you take the book and see if it belongs to you? Whether it does or not, my wish is that the Blue Flower may grow in the garden where you work.

Avalon,
December 1, 1902.

CONTENTS

ILLUSTRATIONS

THE BLUE FLOWER

THE BLUE FLOWER

THE parents were abed and sleeping. The clock
on the wall ticked loudly and lazily, as if it had
time to spare. Outside the rattling windows there
was a restless, whispering wind. The room grew
light, and dark, and wondrous light again,
as the moon played hide-and-seek through the
clouds. The boy, wide-awake and quiet in his bed,
was thinking of the Stranger and his stories.

"It was not what he told me about the treasures," he said to himself, "that was not the thing
which filled me with so strange a longing. I am not
greedy for riches. But the Blue Flower is what I
long for. I can think of nothing else. Never have
I felt so before. It seems as if I had been dreaming
until now—or as if I had just slept over into a
new world.

" Who cared for flowers in the old world where
I used to live? I never heard of anyone whose
whole heart was set upon finding a flower. But now
I cannot even tell all that I feel—sometimes as

happy as if I were enchanted. But when the flower fades from me, when I cannot see it in my mind, then it is like being very thirsty and all alone. That is what the other people could not understand.

"Once upon a time, they say, the animals and the trees and the flowers used to talk to people. It seems to me, every minute, as if they were just going to begin again. When I look at them I can see what they want to say. There must be a great many words that I do not know; if I knew more of them perhaps I could understand things better. I used to love to dance, but now I like better to think after the music."

Gradually the boy lost himself in sweet fancies, and suddenly he found himself again, in the charmed land of sleep. He wandered in far countries, rich and strange; he traversed wild waters with incredible swiftness; marvellous creatures appeared and vanished; he lived with all sorts of men, in battles, in whirling crowds, in lonely huts. He was cast into prison. He fell into dire distress and want. All experiences seemed to be sharpened to an edge. He felt them keenly, yet they did not harm him. He died and came alive again; he loved to the height of passion, and then was parted forever from his beloved. At last, toward morning, as the dawn was stealing near, his soul grew calm, and the pictures showed more clear and firm.

It seemed as if he were walking alone through the deep woods. Seldom the daylight shimmered through the green veil. Soon he came to a rocky gorge in the mountains. Under the mossy stones in the bed of the stream, he heard the water secretly tinkling downward, ever downward, as he climbed upward.

The forest grew thinner and lighter. He came to a fair meadow on the slope of the mountain. Beyond the meadow was a high cliff, and in the face of the cliff an opening like the entrance to a path. Dark was the way, but smooth, and he followed easily on till he came near to a vast cavern from which a flood of radiance streamed to meet him.

As he entered he beheld a mighty beam of light which sprang from the ground, shattering itself against the roof in countless sparks, falling and flowing all together into a great pool in the rock.

Brighter was the light-beam than molten gold, but silent in its rise, and silent in its fall. The sacred stillness of a shrine, a never-broken hush of joy and wonder, filled the cavern. Cool was the dripping radiance that softly trickled down the walls, and the light that rippled from them was pale blue.

But the pool, as the boy drew near and watched it, quivered and glanced with the ever-changing colours of a liquid opal. He dipped his hands in it and wet his lips. It seemed as if a lively breeze passed through his heart.

He felt an irresistible desire to bathe in the pool. Slipping off his clothes he plunged in. It was as if he bathed in a cloud of sunset. A celestial rapture flowed through him. The waves of the stream were like a bevy of nymphs taking shape around him, clinging to him with tender breasts, as he floated onward, lost in delight, yet keenly sensitive to every impression. Swiftly the current bore him out of the pool, into a hollow in the cliff. Here a dimness of slumber shadowed his eyes, while he felt the pressure of the loveliest dreams.

When he awoke again, he was aware of a new

fulness of light, purer and steadier than the first radiance. He found himself lying on the green turf, in the open air, beside a little fountain, which sparkled up and melted away in silver spray. Dark-blue were the rocks that rose at a little distance, veined with white as if strange words were written upon them. Dark-blue was the sky, and cloudless.

All passion had dissolved away from him; every sound was music; every breath was peace; the rocks were like sentinels protecting him; the sky was like a cup of blessing full of tranquil light.

But what charmed him most, and drew him with resistless power, was a tall, clear-blue flower, growing beside the spring, and almost touching him with its broad, glistening leaves. Round about were many other flowers, of all hues. Their odours mingled in a perfect chord of fragrance. He saw nothing but the Blue Flower.

Long and tenderly he gazed at it, with unspeakable love. At last he felt that he must go a little nearer to it, when suddenly it began to move and change. The leaves glistened more brightly, and drew themselves up closely around the swiftly growing stalk. The flower bent itself toward him, and the petals showed a blue, spreading necklace of sapphires, out of which the lovely face of a girl smiled softly into his eyes. His sweet astonishment grew with the wondrous transformation.

All at once he heard his mother's voice calling him, and awoke in his parents' room, already flooded with the gold of the morning sun.

From the German of Novalis.

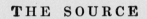

THE SOURCE

THE SOURCE

I

IN the middle of the land that is called by its inhabitants Koorma, and by strangers the Land of the Half-forgotten, I was toiling all day long through heavy sand and grass as hard as wire. Suddenly, toward evening, I came upon a place where a gate opened in the wall of mountains, and the plain ran in through the gate, making a little bay of level country among the hills.

Now this bay was not brown and hard and dry, like the mountains above me, neither was it covered with tawny billows of sand like the desert along the edge of which I had wearily coasted. But the surface of it was smooth and green; and as the winds of twilight breathed across it they were followed by soft waves of verdure, with silvery turnings of the under sides of many leaves, like ripples on a quiet harbour. There were fields of corn, filled with silken rustling, and vineyards with long rows of trimmed maple-trees standing each one like an emerald goblet wreathed with vines, and flower-gardens as bright as if the earth had been embroidered with threads of blue and scarlet and gold, and olive-orchards frosted over with delicate and fragrant blossoms. Red-roofed cottages were scattered everywhere through the sea of greenery, and in the centre, like a white ship surrounded by a flock of little boats, rested a small, fair, shining city.

I wondered greatly how this beauty had come into being on the border of the desert. Passing through the fields and gardens and orchards, I found that they were all encircled and lined with channels full of running water. I followed up one of the smaller channels until it came to a larger stream, and as I walked on beside it, still going upward, it guided me into the midst of the city, where I saw a sweet, merry river flowing through the main street, with abundance of water and a very pleasant sound.

There were houses and shops and lofty palaces and all that makes a city, but the life and joy of all, and the one thing that I remember best, was

12

the river. For in the open square at the edge of the city there were marble pools where the children might bathe and play; at the corners of the streets and on the sides of the houses there were fountains for the drawing of water; at every crossing a stream was turned aside to run out to the vineyards; and the river was the mother of them all.

There were but few people in the streets, and none of the older folk from whom I might ask counsel or a lodging; so I stood and knocked at the door of a house. It was opened by an old man, who greeted me with kindness and bade me enter as his guest. After much courteous entertainment, and when supper was ended, his friendly manner and something of singular attractiveness in his countenance led me to tell him of my strange journeyings in the land of Koorma and in other lands where I had been seeking the Blue Flower, and to inquire of him the name and the story of his city and the cause of the river which made it glad.

"My son," he answered, "this is the city which was called Ablis, that is to say, Forsaken. For long ago men lived here, and the river made their fields fertile, and their dwellings were full of plenty and peace. But because of many evil things which have been half-forgotten, the river was turned aside, or else it was dried up at its source in the high place among the mountains, so that the water flowed down no more. The channels and the trenches and the marble pools and the basins beside the houses remained, but they were empty. So the gardens withered; the fields were barren; the city was desolate; and in the broken cisterns there was scanty water.

"Then there came one from a distant country who was very sorrowful to see the desolation. He told the people that it was vain to dig new cisterns and to keep the channels and trenches clean; for the water had come only from above. The Source must be found again and reopened. The river would not flow unless they traced it back to the spring, and visited it continually, and offered prayers and praises beside it without ceasing. Then the spring would rise to an outpouring, and the water would run down plentifully to make the gardens blossom and the city rejoice.

14

"So he went forth to open the fountain; but there were few that went with him, for he was a poor man of lowly aspect, and the path upward was steep and rough. But his companions saw that as he climbed among the rocks little streams of water gushed from the places where he trod, and pools began to gather in the dry river-bed. He went more swiftly than they could follow him, and at length he passed out of their sight. A little farther on they came to the rising of the river and there, beside the overflowing Source, they found their leader lying dead."

"That was a strange thing," I cried, "and very pitiful. Tell me how it came to pass, and what was the meaning of it."

"I cannot tell the whole of the meaning," replied the old man, after a little pause, "for it was many years ago. But this poor man had many enemies in the city, chiefly among the makers of cisterns, who hated him for his words. I believe that they went out after him secretly and slew him. But his followers came back to the city; and as they came the river began to run down very gently after them. They returned to the Source day by day, bringing others with them; for they said that their leader was really alive, though the form of his life had changed, and that he met them in that high place while they remembered him and prayed and sang songs of praise. More and more the people learned to go with them, and the path grew plainer and easier to find. The more the Source was revisited, the more abundant it became, and the more it filled the river. All the channels and the basins were supplied with water, and men made new channels which were also filled. Some of those who were diggers of trenches and hewers of cisterns said that it was their work which had wrought the change. But the wisest and best among the people knew that it all came from the Source, and they taught that if it should ever again be forgotten and left unvisited the river would fail again and desolation return. So every day, from the gardens and orchards and the streets of the city, men and women and children have gone up the mountain-path with singing, to rejoice beside the spring from which the river flows and to remember the one who opened it. We call it the River Carita. And the name of the city is no more Ablis, but Saloma, which is Peace. And the name of him who died to find the Source for us is so dear that we speak it only when we pray.

"But there are many things yet to learn about our city, and some that seem dark and cast a shadow on my thoughts. Therefore, my son, I bid you to be my guest, for there is a room in my house for the stranger; and to-morrow and on the following days you shall see how life goes with us, and read, if you can, the secret of the city."

That night I slept well, as one who has heard a pleasant tale, with the murmur of running water woven through my dreams; and the next day I went out early into the streets, for I was curious to see the manner of the visitation of the Source.

Already the people were coming forth and turning their steps upward in the mountain-path beside the river. Some of them went alone, swiftly and in silence; others were in groups of two or three, talking as they went; others were in larger companies, and they sang together very gladly and sweetly. But there were many people who remained working in their fields or in their houses, or stayed talking on the corners of the streets. Therefore I joined myself to one of the men who walked alone and asked him why all the people did not go to the spring, since the life of the city depended upon it, and whether, perhaps, the way was so long and so hard that none but the strongest could undertake it.

"Sir," said he, "I perceive that you are a stranger, for the way is both short and easy, so that the children are those who most delight in it; and if a man were in great haste he could go there and return in a little while. But of those who remain behind, some are the busy ones who must visit the fountain at another hour; and some are the careless ones who take life as it comes and never think where it comes from; and some are those who do not believe in the Source and will hear nothing about it."

"How can that be?" I said; "do they not drink of the water, and does it not make their fields green?"

"It is true," he said; "but these men have made wells close by the river, and they say that these wells fill themselves; and they have digged channels through their gardens, and they say that these channels would always have water in them even though the spring should cease to flow. Some of them say also that it is an unworthy thing to drink from a source that another has opened, and that every man ought to find a new spring for himself; so they spend the hour of the visitation, and many more, in searching among the mountains where there is no path."

While I wondered over this, we kept on in the way. There was already quite a throng of people all going in the same direction. And when we came to the Source, which flowed from an opening in a cliff, almost like a chamber hewn in the rock, and made a little garden of wild-flowers around it as it fell, I heard the music of many voices and the beautiful name of him who had given his life to find the forgotten spring.

Then we came down again, singly and in groups, following the river. It seemed already more bright and full and joyous. As we passed through the gardens I saw men turning aside to make new channels through fields which were not yet cultivated. And as we entered the city I saw the wheels of the mills that ground the corn whirling more swiftly, and the maidens coming with their pitchers to draw from the brimming basins at the street corners, and the children laughing because the marble pools were so full that they could swim in them. There was plenty of water everywhere.

For many weeks I stayed in the city of Saloma, going up the mountain-path in the morning, and returning to the day of work and the evening of play. I found friends among the people of the city, not only among those who walked together in the visitation of the Source, but also among those who remained behind, for many of them were kind and generous, faithful in their work, and very pleasant in their conversation.

Yet there was something lacking between me and them. I came not onto firm ground with them, for all their warmth of welcome and their pleasant ways. They were by nature of the race of those who dwell ever in one place; even in their thoughts they went not far abroad. But I have been ever a seeker, and the world seems to me made to wander in, rather than to abide in one corner of it and never see what the rest has in store. Now this was what the people of Saloma could not understand, and for this reason I seemed to them always a stranger, an alien, a guest. The fixed circle of their life was like an invisible wall, and with the best will in the world they knew not how to draw me within it. And I, for my part, while I understood well their wish to rest and be at peace, could not quite understand the way in which it found fulfilment, nor share the repose which seemed to them all-sufficient and lasting. In their gardens I saw ever the same flowers, and none perfect. At their feasts I tasted ever the same food, and none that made an end of hunger. In their talk I heard ever the same words, and none that went to the depth of thought. The very quietude and fixity of their being perplexed and estranged me. What to them was permanent, to me was transient. They were inhabitants: I was a visitor.

THE BLUE FLOWER

The one in all the city of Saloma with whom
I was most at home was Ruamie, the little grand-
daughter of the old man with whom I lodged. To
her, a girl of thirteen, fair-eyed and full of joy,
the wonted round of life had not yet grown to
be a matter of course. She was quick to feel and
answer the newness of every day that dawned.
When a strange bird flew down from the mountains into the gardens, it was she that saw it and
wondered at it. It was she that walked with me
most often in the path to the Source. She went
out with me to the fields in the morning and almost every day found wild-flowers that were new
to me. At sunset she drew me to happy games of
youths and children, where her fancy was never
tired of weaving new turns to the familiar pas-
times. In the dusk she would sit beside me in an
arbour of honeysuckle and question me about the
flower that I was seeking,—for to her I had often
spoken of my quest.

"Is it blue," she asked, "as blue as the speedwell that grows beside the brook?"

"Yes, it is as much bluer than the speedwell, as
the river is deeper than the brook."

"And is it bright," she asked, "as bright as the drops of dew that shine in the moonlight?"

"Yes, it is as much brighter than the drops of dew as the sun is clearer than the moon."

"And is it sweet," she asked, "as sweet as the honeysuckle when the day is warm and still?"

"Yes, it is as much sweeter than the honeysuckle as the night is stiller and more sweet than the day."

"Tell me again," she asked, "when you saw it, and why do you seek it?"

"Once I saw it when I was a boy, no older than you. Our house looked out toward the hills, far away and at sunset softly blue against the eastern sky. It was the day that we laid my father to rest in the little burying-ground among the cedar-trees. There was his father's grave, and his father's father's grave, and there were the places for my mother and for my two brothers and for my sister and for me. I counted them all, when the others had gone back to the house. I paced up and down alone, measuring the ground; there was room enough for us all; and in the western corner where a young elm-tree was growing,—that would be my place, for I was the youngest. How tall would the elm-tree be then? I had never thought of it before. It seemed to make me sad and restless,—wishing for something, I knew not what,—longing to see the world and to taste happiness before I must sleep beneath the elm-tree. Then I looked off to the blue hills, shadowy and dreamlike, the boundary of the little world that I knew. And there, in a cleft between the highest peaks I saw a wondrous thing: for the place at which I was looking seemed to come nearer and nearer to me; I saw the trees, the rocks, the ferns, the white road winding before me; the enfolding hills unclosed like leaves, and in the heart of them I saw a Blue Flower, so bright, so beautiful that my eyes filled with tears as I looked. It was like a face that smiled at me and promised something. Then I heard a call, like the note of a trumpet very far away, calling me to come. And as I listened the flower faded into the dimness of the hills."

"Did you follow it," asked Ruamie, "and did

24

you go away from your home? How could you do that?"

"Yes, Ruamie, when the time came, as soon as I was free, I set out on my journey, and my home is at the end of the journey, wherever that may be."

"And the flower," she asked, "you have seen it again?"

"Once again, when I was a youth, I saw it. After a long voyage upon stormy seas, we came into a quiet haven, and there the friend who was dearest to me, said good-by, for he was going back to his own country and his father's house, but I was still journeying onward. So as I stood at the bow of the ship, sailing out into the wide blue water, far away among the sparkling waves I saw a little island, with shores of silver sand and slopes of fairest green, and in the middle of the island the Blue Flower was growing, wondrous tall and dazzling, brighter than the sapphire of the sea. Then the call of the distant trumpet came floating across the water, and while it was sounding a shimmer of fog swept over the island and I could see it no more."

"Was it a real island," asked Ruamie. "Did you ever find it?"

"Never; for the ship sailed another way. But once again I saw the flower; three days before I came to Saloma. It was on the edge of the desert, close under the shadow of the great mountains. A vast loneliness was round about me; it seemed as if I was the only soul living upon earth; and I longed for the dwellings of men. Then as I woke in the morning I looked up at the dark ridge of the mountains, and there against the brightening blue of the sky I saw the Blue Flower standing up clear and brave. It shone so deep and pure that the sky grew pale around it. Then the echo of the far-off trumpet drifted down the hillsides, and the sun rose, and the flower was melted away in light. So I rose and travelled on till I came to Saloma."

"And now," said the child, "you are at home with us. Will you not stay for a long, long while? You may find the Blue Flower here. There are many kinds in the fields. I find new ones every day."

"I will stay while I can, Ruamie," I answered,

taking her hand in mine as we walked back to the house at nightfall, "but how long that may be I cannot tell. For with you I am at home, yet the place where I must abide is the place where the flower grows, and when the call comes I must follow it."

"Yes," said she, looking at me half in doubt, "I think I understand. But wherever you go I hope you will find the flower at last."

In truth there were many things in the city that troubled me and made me restless, in spite of the sweet comfort of Ruamie's friendship and the tranquillity of the life in Saloma. I came to see the meaning of what the old man had said about the shadow that rested upon his thoughts. For there were some in the city who said that the hours of visitation were wasted, and that it would be better to employ the time in gathering water from the pools that formed among the mountains in the rainy season, or in sinking wells along the edge of the desert. Others had newly come to the city and were teaching that there was no Source, and that the story of the poor man who reopened it was a fable, and that the hours of visitation were only hours of dreaming. There were many who believed them, and many more who said that it did not matter whether their words were true or false, and that it was of small moment whether men went to visit the fountain or not, provided only that they worked in the gardens and kept the marble pools and basins in repair and opened new canals through the fields, since there always had been and always would be plenty of water.

As I listened to these sayings it seemed to me doubtful what the end of the city would be. And while this doubt was yet heavy upon me, I heard at midnight the faint calling of the trumpet, sounding along the crest of the mountains: and as I went out to look where it came from, I saw, through the glimmering veil of the milky way, the shape of a blossom of celestial blue, whose petals seemed to fall and fade as I looked. So I bade farewell to the old man in whose house I had learned to love the hour of visitation and the Source and the name of him who opened it; and I kissed the hands and the brow of the little

Ruamie who had entered my heart, and went forth sadly from the land of Koorma into other lands, to look for the Blue Flower.

II

In the Book of the Voyage without a Harbour is written the record of the ten years which passed before I came back again to the city of Saloma.

It was not easy to find, for I came down through the mountains, and as I looked from a distant shoulder of the hills for the little bay full of greenery, it was not to be seen. There was only a white town shining far off against the brown cliffs, like a flake of mica in a cleft of the rocks. Then I slept that night, full of care, on the hillside, and rising before dawn, came down in the early morning toward the city.

The fields were lying parched and yellow under the sunrise, and great cracks gaped in the earth as if it were thirsty. The trenches and channels were still there, but there was little water in them;

and through the ragged fringes of the rusty vineyards I heard, instead of the cheerful songs of
the vintagers, the creaking of dry windlasses and
the hoarse throb of the pumps in sunken wells.
The girdle of gardens had shrunk like a wreath
of withered flowers, and all the bright embroidery
of earth was faded to a sullen gray.

At the foot of an ancient, leafless olive-tree I
saw a group of people kneeling around a newly
opened well. I asked a man who was digging beside the dusty path what this might mean. He
straightened himself for a moment, wiping the
sweat from his brow, and answered, sullenly, "They
are worshipping the windlass: how else should they
bring water into their fields?" Then he fell furiously to digging again, and I passed on into the
city.

There was no sound of murmuring streams in
the streets, and down the main bed of the river I
saw only a few shallow puddles, joined together
by a slowly trickling thread. Even these were
fenced and guarded so that no one might come
near to them, and there were men going among

the houses with water-skins on their shoulders, crying "Water! Water to sell!"

The marble pools in the open square were
empty; and at one of them there was a crowd looking at a man who was being beaten with rods. A
bystander told me that the officers of the city had
ordered him to be punished because he had said
that the pools and the basins and the channels
were not all of pure marble, without a flaw. "For
this," said he, "is the evil doctrine that has come
in to take away the glory of our city, and because
of this the water has failed."

"It is a sad change," I answered, "and doubtless they who have caused it should suffer more
than others. But can you tell me at what hour and
in what manner the people now observe the visitation of the Source?"

He looked curiously at me and replied: "I do
not understand you. There is no visitation save the
inspection of the cisterns and the wells which the
syndics of the city, whom we call the Princes of
Water, carry on daily at every hour. What source
is this of which you speak?"

So I went on through the street, where all the passers-by seemed in haste and wore weary countenances, until I came to the house where I had lodged. There was a little basin here against the wall, with a slender stream of water still flowing into it, and a group of children standing near with their pitchers, waiting to fill them.

The door of the house was closed; but when I knocked, it opened and a maiden came forth. She was pale and sad in aspect, but a light of joy dawned over the snow of her face, and I knew by the youth in her eyes that it was Ruamie, who had walked with me through the vineyards long ago.

With both hands she welcomed me, saying: "You are expected. Have you found the Blue Flower?"

"Not yet," I answered, "but something drew me back to you. I would know how it fares with you, and I would go again with you to visit the Source."

At this her face grew bright, but with a tender, half-sad brightness.

"The Source!" she said. "Ah, yes, I was sure

32

that you would remember it. And this is the hour of the visitation. Come, let us go up together."

Then we went alone through the busy and weary multitudes of the city toward the mountain-path. So forsaken was it and so covered with stones and overgrown with wire-grass that I could not have found it but for her guidance. But as we climbed upward the air grew clearer, and more sweet, and I questioned her of the things that had come to pass in my absence. I asked her of the kind old man who had taken me into his house when I came as a stranger. She said, softly, "He is dead."

"And where are the men and women, his friends, who once thronged this pathway? Are they also dead?"

"They also are dead."

"But where are the younger ones who sang here so gladly as they marched upward? Surely they are living?"

"They have forgotten."

"Where then are the young children whose fathers taught them this way and bade them remember it. Have they forgotten?"

"They have forgotten."

"But why have you alone kept the hour of visitation? Why have you not turned back with your companions? How have you walked here solitary day after day?"

She turned to me with a divine regard, and laying her hand gently over mine, she said, "I remember always."

Then I saw a few wild-flowers blossoming beside the path.

We drew near to the Source, and entered into the chamber hewn in the rock. She kneeled and bent over the sleeping spring. She murmured again and again the beautiful name of him who had died to find it. Her voice repeated the song that had once been sung by many voices. Her tears fell softly on the spring, and as they fell it seemed as if the water stirred and rose to meet her bending face, and when she looked up it was as if the dew had fallen on a flower.

We came very slowly down the path along the river Carita, and rested often beside it, for surely, I thought, the rising of the spring had sent a

She murmured again and again the beautiful name.

little more water down its dry bed, and some of it must flow on to the city. So it was almost evening when we came back to the streets. The people were hurrying to and fro, for it was the day before the choosing of new Princes of Water; and there was much dispute about them, and strife over the building of new cisterns to hold the stores of rain which might fall in the next year. But none cared for us, as we passed by like strangers, and we came unnoticed to the door of the house.

Then a great desire of love and sorrow moved within my breast, and I said to Ruamie, "You are the life of the city, for you alone remember. Its secret is in your heart, and your faithful keeping of the hours of visitation is the only cause why the river has not failed altogether and the curse of desolation returned. Let me stay with you, sweet soul of all the flowers that are dead, and I will cherish you forever. Together we will visit the Source every day; and we shall turn the people, by our lives and by our words, back to that which they have forgotten."

There was a smile in her eyes so deep that its

meaning cannot be spoken, as she lifted my hand to her lips, and answered,

"Not so, dear friend, for who can tell whether life or death will come to the city, whether its people will remember at last, or whether they will forget forever. Its lot is mine, for I was born here, and here my life is rooted. But you are of the Children of the Unquiet Heart, whose feet can never rest until their task of errors is completed and their lesson of wandering is learned to the end. Until then go forth, and do not forget that I shall remember always."

Behind her quiet voice I heard the silent call that compels us, and passed down the street as one walking in a dream. At the place where the path turned aside to the ruined vineyards I looked back. The low sunset made a circle of golden rays about her head and a strange twin blossom of celestial blue seemed to shine in her tranquil eyes.

Since then I know not what has befallen the city, nor whether it is still called Saloma, or once more Ablis, which is Forsaken. But if it lives at all, I know that it is because there is one there who remembers, and keeps the hour of visitation, and treads the steep way, and breathes the beautiful name over the spring, and sometimes I think that long before my seeking and journeying brings me to the Blue Flower, it will bloom for Ruamie beside the still waters of the Source.

THE MILL

THE MILL

I

*How the Young Martimor would Become a Knight
and Assay Great Adventure*

WHEN Sir Lancelot was come out of the Red
Launds where he did many deeds of arms, he rested
him long with play and game in a land that is
called Beausejour. For in that land there are
neither castles nor enchantments, but many fair
manors, with orchards and fields lying about them;
and the people that dwell therein have good cheer
continually.

Of the wars and of the strange quests that are
ever afoot in Northgalis and Lionesse and the Out
Isles, they hear nothing; but are well content to
till the earth in summer when the world is green;
and when the autumn changes green to gold they
pitch pavilions among the fruit-trees and the vineyards, making merry with song and dance while
they gather harvest of corn and apples and

grapes; and in the white days of winter for pastime they have music of divers instruments and the playing of pleasant games.

But of the telling of tales in that land there is little skill, neither do men rightly understand the singing of ballads and romaunts. For one year there is like another, and so their life runs away, and they leave the world to God.

Then Sir Lancelot had great ease for a time in this quiet land, and often he lay under the apple-trees sleeping, and again he taught the people new games and feats of skill. For into what place soever he came he was welcome, though the inhabitants knew not his name and great renown, nor the famous deeds that he had done in tournament and battle. Yet for his own sake, because he was a very gentle knight, fair-spoken and full of courtesy and a good man of his hands withal, they doted upon him.

So he began to tell them tales of many things that have been done in the world by clean knights and faithful squires. Of the wars against the Saracens and misbelieving men; of the discomfiture of

the Romans when they came to take truage of
King Arthur; of the strife with the eleven kings
and the battle that was ended but never finished;
of the Questing Beast and how King Pellinore and
then Sir Palamides followed it; of Balin that gave
the dolourous stroke unto King Pellam; of Sir Tor
that sought the lady's brachet and by the way
overcame two knights and smote off the head of the
outrageous caitiff Abelleus,—of these and many
like matters of pith and moment, full of blood and
honour, told Sir Lancelot, and the people had mar-
vel of his words.

Now, among them that listened to him gladly,
was a youth of good blood and breeding, very fair
in the face and of great stature. His name was
Martimor. Strong of arm was he, and his neck
was like a pillar. His legs were as tough as beams
of ash-wood, and in his heart was the hunger of
noble tatches and deeds. So when he heard of Sir
Lancelot these redoubtable histories he was taken
with desire to assay his strength. And he besought
the knight that they might joust together.

But in the land of Beausejour there were no

arms of war save such as Sir Lancelot had brought
with him. Wherefore they made shift to fashion a
harness out of kitchen gear, with a brazen platter
for a breast-plate, and the cover of the greatest of
all kettles for a shield, and for a helmet a round
pot of iron, whereof the handle stuck down at
Martimor's back like a tail. And for spear he got
him a stout young fir-tree, the point hardened in
the fire, and Sir Lancelot lent to him the sword that
he had taken from the false knight that distressed
all ladies.

Thus was Martimor accoutred for the jousting,
and when he had climbed upon his horse, there
arose much laughter and mockage. Self Sir Lancelot laughed a little, though he was ever a grave
man, and said, "Now must we call this knight, *La
Queue de Fer*, by reason of the tail at his back."

But Martimor was half merry and half wroth,
and crying " 'Ware!" he dressed his spear beneath
his arm. Right so he rushed upon Sir Lancelot, and
so marvellously did his harness jangle and smite together as he came, that the horse of Sir Lancelot
was frighted and turned aside. Thus the point of

the fir-tree caught him upon the shoulder and
came near to unhorse him. Then Martimor drew
rein and shouted: "Ha! ha! has Iron-Tail done
well?"

"Nobly hast thou done," said Lancelot, laughing, the while he amended his horse, "but let not
the first stroke turn thy head, else will the tail of
thy helmet hang down afore thee and mar the second stroke!"

So he kept his horse in hand and guided him
warily, making feint now on this side and now on
that, until he was aware that the youth grew hot
with the joy of fighting and sought to deal with
him roughly and bigly. Then he cast aside his
spear and drew sword, and as Martimor walloped
toward him, he lightly swerved, and with one
stroke cut in twain the young fir-tree, so that not
above an ell was left in the youth's hand.

Then was the youth full of fire, and he also drew
sword and made at Sir Lancelot, lashing heavily as
he would hew down a tree. But the knight guarded and warded without distress, until the other
breathed hard and was blind with sweat. Then

Lancelot smote him with a mighty stroke upon the head, but with the flat of his sword, so that Martimor's breath went clean out of him, and the blood gushed from his mouth, and he fell over the croup of his horse as he were a man slain.

Then Sir Lancelot laughed no more, but grieved, for he weened that he had harmed the youth, and he liked him passing well. So he ran to him and held him in his arms fast and tended him. And when the breath came again into his body, Lancelot was glad, and desired the youth that he would pardon him of that unequal joust and of the stroke too heavy.

At this Martimor sat up and took him by the hand. "Pardon?" he cried. "No talk of pardon between thee and me, my Lord Lancelot! Thou hast given me such joy of my life as never I had before. It made me glad to feel thy might. And now am I delibred and fully concluded that I also will become a knight, and thou shalt instruct me how and in what land I shall seek great adventure."

II

How Martimor was Instructed of Sir Lancelot to Set Forth Upon His Quest

So right gladly did Sir Lancelot advise the young Martimor of all the customs and vows of the noble order of knighthood, and shew how he might become a well-ruled and a hardy knight to win good fame and renown. For between these two from the first there was close brotherhood and affiance, though in years and in breeding they were so far apart, and this brotherhood endured until the last, as ye shall see, nor was the affiance broken.

Thus willingly learned the youth of his master; being instructed first in the art and craft to manage and guide a horse; then to handle the shield and the spear, and both to cut and to foin with the sword; and last of all in the laws of honour and courtesy, whereby a man may rule his own spirit and so obtain grace of God, praise of princes, and favour of fair ladies.

"For this I tell thee," said Sir Lancelot, as they sat together under an apple-tree, "there be many good fighters that are false knights, breaking faith with man and woman, envious, lustful and orgulous. In them courage is cruel, and love is lecherous. And in the end they shall come to shame and shall be overcome by a simpler knight than themselves; or else they shall win sorrow and despite by the slaying of better men than they be; and with their paramours they shall have weary dole and distress of soul and body; for he that is false, to him shall none be true, but all things shall be unhappy about him."

"But how and if a man be true in heart," said Martimor, "yet by some enchantment, or evil fortune, he may do an ill deed and one that is harmful to his lord or to his friend, even as Balin and his brother Balan slew each the other unknown?"

"That is in God's hand," said Lancelot. "Doubtless he may pardon and assoil all such in their unhappiness, forasmuch as the secret of it is with him."

"And how if a man be entangled in love," said

Martimor, "yet his love be set upon one that is not lawful for him to have? For either he must deny his love, which is great shame, or else he must do dishonour to the law. What shall he then do?"

At this Sir Lancelot was silent, and heaved a great sigh. Then said he: "Rest assured that this man shall have sorrow enough. For out of this net he may not escape, save by falsehood on the one side, or by treachery on the other. Therefore say I that he shall not assay to escape, but rather right manfully to bear the bonds with which he is bound, and to do honour to them."

"How may this be?" said Martimor.

"By clean living," said Lancelot, "and by keeping himself from wine which heats the blood, and by quests and labours and combats wherein the fierceness of the heart is spent and overcome, and by inward joy in the pure worship of his lady, whereat none may take offence."

"How then shall a man bear himself in the following of a quest?" said Martimor. "Shall he set his face ever forward, and turn not to right, or left, whatever meet him by the way? Or shall he hold himself ready to answer them that call to him, and to succour them that ask help of him, and to turn aside from his path for rescue and good service?"

"Enough of questions!" said Lancelot. "These are things whereto each man must answer for himself, and not for other. True knight taketh counsel of the time. Every day his own deed. And the winning of a quest is not by haste, nor by hap, but what needs to be done, that must ye do while ye are in the way."

Then because of the love that Sir Lancelot bore to Martimor he gave him his own armour, and the good spear wherewith he had unhorsed many knights, and the sword that he took from Sir Peris de Forest Savage that distressed all ladies, but his shield he gave not, for therein his own remembrance was blazoned. So he let make a new shield, and in the corner was painted a Blue Flower that was nameless, and this he gave to Martimor, saying: "Thou shalt name it when thou hast found it, and so shalt thou have both crest and motto."

"Now am I well beseen," cried Martimor, "and

50

my adventures are before me. Which way shall I ride, and where shall I find them?"

"Ride into the wind," said Lancelot, "and what chance soever it blows thee, thereby do thy best, as it were the first and the last. Take not thy hand from it until it be fulfilled. So shalt thou most quickly and worthily achieve knighthood."

Then they embraced like brothers; and each bade other keep him well; and Sir Lancelot in leather jerkin, with naked head, but with his shield and sword, rode to the south toward Camelot; and Martimor rode into the wind, westward, over the hill.

III

How Martimor Came to the Mill and There was Stayed in a Delay

So by wildsome ways in strange countries and through many waters and valleys rode Martimor forty days, but adventure met him none, blow the wind never so fierce or fickle. Neither dragons, nor giants, nor false knights, nor distressed ladies, nor fays, nor kings imprisoned could he find.

"These are ill times for adventure," said he, "the world is full of meat and sleepy. Now must I ride farther afield and undertake some ancient, famous quest wherein other knights have failed and fallen. Either I shall follow the Questing Beast with Sir Palamides, or I shall find Merlin at the great stone whereunder the Lady of the Lake enchanted him and deliver him from that enchantment, or I shall assay the cleansing of the Forest Perilous, or I shall win the favour of La Belle Dame Sans Merci, or mayhap I shall adventure the quest of the Sangreal. One or other of these will I achieve, or bleed the best blood of my body." Thus pondering and dreaming he came by the road down a gentle hill with close woods on either hand; and so into a valley with a swift river flowing through it; and on the river a Mill.

So white it stood among the trees, and so merrily whirred the wheel as the water turned it, and so bright blossomed the flowers in the garden, that Martimor had joy of the sight, for it minded him of his own country. "But here is no adventure," thought he, and made to ride by.

Even then came a young maid suddenly through the garden crying and wringing her hands. And when she saw him she cried him help. At this Martimor alighted quickly and ran into the garden, where the young maid soon led him to the millpond, which was great and deep, and made him understand that her little hound was swept away by the water and was near to perishing.

There saw he a red and white brachet, caught by the swift stream that ran into the race, fast swimming as ever he could swim, yet by no means able to escape. Then Martimor stripped off his harness and leaped into the water and did marvellously to rescue the little hound. But the fierce river dragged his legs, and buffeted him, and hurtled at him, and drew him down, as it were an enemy wrestling with him, so that he had much ado to come where the brachet was, and more to win back again, with the brachet in his arm, to the dry land.

Which when he had done he was clean for-spent and fell upon the ground as a dead man. At this the young maid wept yet more bitterly than she had wept for her hound, and cried aloud, "Alas, if so goodly a man should spend his life for my little brachet!" So she took his head upon her knee and cherished him and beat the palms of his hands, and the hound licked his face. And when Martimor opened his eyes he saw the face of the maid that it was fair as any flower.

Then was she shamed, and put him gently from her knee, and began to thank him and to ask with what she might reward him for the saving of the brachet.

"A night's lodging and a day's cheer," quoth Martimor.

"As long as thee liketh," said she, "for my father, the miller, will return ere sundown, and right gladly will he have a guest so brave."

"Longer might I like," said he, "but longer may I not stay, for I ride in a quest and seek great adventures to become a knight."

So they bestowed the horse in the stable, and went into the Mill; and when the miller was come home they had such good cheer with eating of venison and pan-cakes, and drinking of hydromel, and singing of pleasant ballads, that Martimor clean forgot he was in a delay. And going to his bed in a fair garret he dreamed of the Maid of the Mill, whose name was Lirette.

IV

How the Mill was in Danger and the Delay Endured

IN the morning Martimor lay late and thought large thoughts of his quest, and whither it might lead him, and to what honour it should bring him. As he dreamed thus, suddenly he heard in the hall below a trampling of feet and a shouting, with the voice of Lirette crying and shrieking. With that he sprang out of his bed, and caught up his sword and dagger, leaping lightly and fiercely down the stair.

There he saw three foul churls, whereof two strove with the miller, beating him with great clubs, while the third would master the Maid and drag her away to do her shame, but she fought shrewdly. Then Martimor rushed upon the churls, shouting for joy, and there was a great medley of breaking chairs and tables and cursing and smiting, and with his sword he gave horrible strokes.

One of the knaves that fought with the miller, he smote upon the shoulder and clave him to the navel. And at the other he foined fiercely so that the point of the sword went through his back and stuck fast in the wall. But the third knave, that was the biggest and the blackest, and strove to bear away the Maid, left hold of her, and leaped upon Martimor and caught him by the middle and crushed him so that his ribs cracked.

Thus they weltered and wrung together, and now one of them was above and now the other; and ever as they wallowed Martimor smote him with his dagger, but there came forth no blood, only water.

Then the black churl broke away from him and ran out at the door of the mill, and Martimor after. So they ran through the garden to the river, and there the churl sprang into the water, and swept away raging and foaming. And as he went he shouted, "Yet will I put thee to the worse, and mar the Mill, and have the Maid!"

Then Martimor cried, "Never while I live shalt

thou mar the Mill or have the Maid, thou foul, black, misbegotten churl!" So he returned to the Mill, and there the damsel Lirette made him to understand that these three churls were long time enemies of the Mill, and sought ever to destroy it and to do despite to her and her father. One of them was Ignis, and another was Ventus, and these were the twain that he had smitten. But the third, that fled down the river (and he was ever the fiercest and the most outrageous), his name was Flumen, for he dwelt in the caves of the stream, and was the master of it before the Mill was built.

"And now," wept the Maid, "he must have had his will with me and with the Mill, but for God's mercy, thanked be our Lord Jesus!"

"Thank me too," said Martimor.

"So I do," said Lirette, and she kissed him. "Yet am I heavy at heart and fearful, for my father is sorely mishandled and his arm is broken, so that he cannot tend the Mill nor guard it. And Flumen is escaped; surely he will harm us again. Now I know not, where I shall look for help."

"Why not here?" said Martimor.

Then Lirette looked him in the face, smiling a little sorrily. "But thou ridest in a quest," quoth she, "thou mayst not stay from thy adventures."

"A month," said he.

"Till my father be well?" said she.

"A month," said he.

"Till thou hast put Flumen to the worse?" said she.

"Right willingly would I have to do with that base, slippery knave again," said he, "but more than a month I may not stay, for my quest calls me and I must win worship of men or ever I become a knight."

So they bound up the miller's wounds and set the Mill in order. But Martimor had much to do to learn the working of the Mill; and they were busied with the grinding of wheat and rye and barley and divers kinds of grain; and the miller's hurts were mended every day; and at night there was merry rest and good cheer; and Martimor talked with the Maid of the great adventure that he must find; and thus the delay endured in pleasant wise.

THE MILL

V

Yet More of the Mill, and of the Same Delay, also of the Maid

Now at the end of the third month, which was November, Martimor made Lirette to understand that it was high time he should ride farther to follow his quest. For the miller was now recovered, and it was long that they had heard and seen naught of Flumen, and doubtless that black knave was well routed and dismayed that he would not come again. Lirette prayed him and desired him that he would tarry yet one week. But Martimor said, No! for his adventures were before him, and that he could not be happy save in the doing of great deeds and the winning of knightly fame. Then he showed her the Blue Flower in his shield that was nameless, and told her how Sir Lancelot had said that he must find it, then should he name it and have both crest and motto.

"Does it grow in my garden?" said Lirette.

"I have not seen it," said he, "and now the flowers are all faded."

"Perhaps in the month of May?" said she.

"In that month I will come again," said he, "for by that time it may fortune that I shall achieve my quest, but now forth must I fare."

So there was sad cheer in the Mill that day, and at night there came a fierce storm with howling wind and plumping rain, and Martimor slept ill. About the break of day he was wakened by a great roaring and pounding; then he looked out of window, and saw the river in flood, with black waves spuming and raving, like wood beasts, and driving before them great logs and broken trees. Thus the river hurled and hammered at the mill-dam so that it trembled, and the logs leaped as they would spring over it, and the voice of Flumen shouted hoarsely and hungrily, "Yet will I mar the Mill and have the Maid!"

Then Martimor ran with the miller out upon the dam, and they laboured at the gates that held the river back, and thrust away the logs that were heaped over them, and cut with axes, and fought with the river. So at last two of the gates were lifted and one was broken, and the flood ran down ramping and roaring in great raundon, and as it ran the black face of Flumen sprang above it, crying, "Yet will I mar both Mill and Maid."

"That shalt thou never do," cried Martimor, "by foul or fair, while the life beats in my body."

So he came back with the miller into the Mill, and there was meat ready for them and they ate strongly and with good heart. "Now," said the miller, "must I mend the gate. But how it may be done, I know not, for surely this will be great travail for a man alone."

"Why alone?" said Martimor.

"Thou wilt stay, then?" said Lirette.

"Yea," said he.

"For another month?" said she.

"Till the gate be mended," said he.

But when the gate was mended there came another flood and brake the second gate. And when that was mended there came another flood and brake the third gate. So when all three were mended firm and fast, being bound with iron, still the grimly river hurled over the dam, and the voice of Flumen muttered in the dark of winter nights,

"Yet will I mar—mar—mar—yet will I mar Mill and Maid."

"Oho!" said Martimor, "this is a durable and dogged knave. Art thou feared of him Lirette?"

"Not so," said she, "for thou art stronger. But fear have I of the day when thou ridest forth in thy quest."

"Well, as to that," said he, "when I have overcome this false devil Flumen, then will we consider and appoint that day."

So the delay continued, and Martimor was both busy and happy at the Mill, for he liked and loved this damsel well, and was fain of her company. Moreover the strife with Flumen was great joy to him.

VI

How the Month of May came to the Mill, and the Delay was Made Longer

Now when the month of May came to the Mill it brought a plenty of sweet flowers, and Lirette wrought in the garden. With her, when the day was spent and the sun rested upon the edge of the hill, went Martimor, and she showed him all her flowers that were blue. But none of them was like the flower on his shield.

"Is it this?" she cried, giving him a violet.

"Too dark," said he.

"Then here it is," she said, plucking a posy of forget-me-not.

"Too light," said he.

"Surely this is it," and she brought him a spray of blue-bells.

"Too slender," said he, "and well I ween that I may not find that flower, till I ride farther in my quest and achieve great adventure."

Then was the Maid cast down, and Martimor was fain to comfort her.

So while they walked thus in the garden, the days were fair and still, and the river ran lowly and slowly, as it were full of gentleness, and Flumen had amended him of his evil ways. But full of craft and guile was that false foe. For now that the gates were firm and strong, he found a way down through the corner of the dam, where a water-rat had burrowed, and there the water went seeping and creeping, gnawing ever at the hidden breach. Presently in the night came a mizzling rain, and far among the hills a cloud brake open, and the mill-pond flowed over and under, and the dam crumbled away, and the Mill shook, and the whole river ran roaring through the garden.

Then was Martimor wonderly wroth, because the river had blotted out the Maid's flowers. "And one day," she cried, holding fast to him and trembling, "one day Flumen will have me, when thou art gone."

"Not so," said he, "by the faith of my body that foul fiend shall never have thee. I will bind him, I will compel him, or die in the deed."

So he went forth, upward along the river, till he came to a strait place among the hills. There was a great rock full of caves and hollows, and there the water whirled and burbled in furious wise. "Here," thought he, "is the hold of the knave Flumen, and if I may cut through above this rock and make a dyke with a gate in it, to let down the water another way when the floods come, so shall I spoil him of his craft and put him to the worse."

"Surely this is it," and she brought him a spray of blue-bells.

Then he toiled day and night to make the dyke, and ever by night Flumen came and strove with him, and did his power to cast him down and strangle him. But Martimor stood fast and drave him back.

And at last, as they wrestled and whapped together, they fell headlong in the stream.

"Ho-o!" shouted Flumen, "now will I drown thee, and mar the Mill and the Maid."

But Martimor gripped him by the neck and thrust his head betwixt the leaves of the gate and shut them fast, so that his eyes stood out like gobbets of foam, and his black tongue hung from his mouth like a water-weed.

"Now shalt thou swear never to mar Mill nor Maid, but meekly to serve them," cried Martimor.

Then Flumen sware by wind and wave, by storm and stream, by rain and river, by pond and pool, by flood and fountain, by dyke and dam.

"These be changeable things," said Martimor, "swear by the Name of God."

So he sware, and even as the Name passed his teeth, the gobbets of foam floated forth from the gate, and the water-weed writhed away with the stream, and the river flowed fair and softly, with a sound like singing.

Then Martimor came back to the Mill, and told how Flumen was overcome and made to swear a pact. Thus their hearts waxed light and jolly, and they kept that day as it were a love-day.

VII

*How Martimor Bled for a Lady and Lived for a
Maid, and how His Great Adventure Ended
and Began at the Mill*

Now leave we of the Mill and Martimor and the Maid, and let us speak of a certain Lady, passing tall and fair and young. This was the Lady Beau-vivante, that was daughter to King Pellinore. And three false knights took her by craft from her father's court and led her away to work their will on her. But she escaped from them as they slept by a well, and came riding on a white palfrey, over hill and dale, as fast as ever she could drive.

Thus she came to the Mill, and her palfrey was

spent, and there she took refuge, beseeching Martimor that he would hide her, and defend her from those caitiff knights that must soon follow.

"Of hiding," said he, "will I hear naught, but of defending am I full fain. For this have I waited."

Then he made ready his horse and his armour, and took both spear and sword, and stood forth in the bridge. Now this bridge was strait, so that none could pass there but singly, and that not till Martimor yielded or was beaten down.

Then came the three knights that followed the Lady, riding fiercely down the hill. And when they came about ten spear-lengths from the bridge, they halted, and stood still as it had been a plump of wood. One rode in black, and one rode in yellow, and the third rode in black and yellow. So they cried Martimor that he should give them passage, for they followed a quest.

"Passage takes, who passage makes!" cried Martimor. "Right well I know your quest, and it is a foul one."

Then the knight in black rode at him lightly,

but Martimor encountered him with the spear and smote him backward from his horse, that his head struck the coping of the bridge and brake his neck. Then came the knight in yellow, walloping heavily, and him the spear pierced through the midst of the body and burst in three pieces: so he fell on his back and the life went out of him, but the spear stuck fast and stood up from his breast as a stake.

Then the knight in black and yellow, that was as big as both his brethren, gave a terrible shout, and rode at Martimor like a wood lion. But he fended with his shield that the spear went aside, and they clapped together like thunder, and both horses were overthrown. And lightly they avoided their horses and rushed together, tracing, rasing, and foining. Such strokes they gave that great pieces were clipped away from their hauberks, and their helms, and they staggered to and fro like drunken men. Then they hurtled together like rams and each battered other the wind out of his body. So they sat either on one side of the bridge, to take their breath, glaring the one at the other as two owls. Then they stepped together and fought freshly, smiting and thrusting, ramping and reeling, panting, snorting, and scattering blood, for the space of two hours. So the knight in black and yellow, because he was heavier, drave Martimor backward step by step till he came to the crown of the bridge, and there fell grovelling. At this the Lady Beauvivante shrieked and wailed, but the damsel Lirette cried loudly, "Up! Martimor, strike again!"

Then the courage came into his body, and with a great might he abraid upon his feet, and smote the black and yellow knight upon the helm by an overstroke so fierce that the sword sheared away the third part of his head, as it had been a rotten cheese. So he lay upon the bridge, and the blood ran out of him. And Martimor smote off the rest of his head quite, and cast it into the river. Likewise did he with the other twain that lay dead beyond the bridge. And he cried to Flumen, "Hide me these black eggs that hatched evil thoughts." So the river bore them away.

Then Martimor came into the Mill, all for-bled;

69

"Now are ye free, lady," he cried, and fell down in a swoon. Then the Lady and the Maid wept full sore and made great dole and unlaced his helm; and Lirette cherished him tenderly to recover his life.

So while they were thus busied and distressed, came Sir Lancelot with a great company of knights and squires riding for to rescue the princess. When he came to the bridge all bedashed with blood, and the bodies of the knights headless, "Now, by my lady's name," said he, "here has been good fighting, and those three caitiffs are slain! By whose hand I wonder?"

So he came into the Mill, and there he found Martimor recovered of his swoon, and had marvellous joy of him, when he heard how he had wrought.

"Now are thou proven worthy of the noble order of knighthood," said Lancelot, and forthwith he dubbed him knight.

Then he said that Sir Martimor should ride with him to the court of King Pellinore, to receive a castle and a fair lady to wife, for doubtless the

King would deny him nothing to reward the rescue of his daughter.

But Martimor stood in a muse; then said he, "May a knight have his free will and choice of castles, where he will abide?"

"Within the law," said Lancelot, "and by the King's word he may."

"Then choose I the Mill," said Martimor, "for here will I dwell."

"Freely spoken," said Lancelot, laughing, "so art thou Sir Martimor of the Mill; no doubt the King will confirm it. And now what sayest thou of ladies?"

"May a knight have his free will and choice here also?" said he.

"According to his fortune," said Lancelot, "and by the lady's favour, he may."

"Well, then," said Sir Martimor, taking Lirette by the hand, "this Maid is to me liefer to have and to wield as my wife than any dame or princess that is christened."

"What, brother," said Sir Lancelot, "is the wind in that quarter? And will the Maid have thee?"

71

"I will well," said Lirette.

"Now are you well provided," said Sir Lancelot, "with knighthood, and a castle, and a lady. Lacks but a motto and a name for the Blue Flower in thy shield."

"He that names it shall never find it," said Sir Martimor, "and he that finds it needs no name."

So Lirette rejoiced Sir Martimor and loved together during their life-days; and this is the end and the beginning of the Story of the Mill.

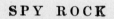

SPY ROCK

SPY ROCK

I

IT must have been near Sutherland's Pond that I lost the way. For there the deserted road which I had been following through the Highlands ran out upon a meadow all abloom with purple loose-strife and golden Saint-John's wort. The declining sun cast a glory over the lonely field, and far in the corner, nigh to the woods, there was a touch of the celestial colour: blue of the sky seen between white clouds: blue of the sea shimmering through faint drifts of silver mist. The hope of finding that hue of distance and mystery embodied in a living form, the old hope of discovering the Blue Flower rose again in my heart. But it was only for a moment, for when I came nearer I saw that the colour which had caught my eye came from a multitude of closed gentians—the blossoms which never open into perfection—growing so closely together that their blended promise had seemed like a single flower.

75

So I harked back again, slanting across the meadow, to find the road. But it had vanished. Wandering among the alders and clumps of gray birches, here and there I found a track that looked like it; but as I tried each one, it grew more faint and uncertain and at last came to nothing in a thicket or a marsh. While I was thus beating about the bush the sun dropped below the western rim of hills. It was necessary to make the most of the lingering light, if I did not wish to be benighted in the woods. The little village of Canterbury, which was the goal of my day's march, must lie about to the north just beyond the edge of the mountain, and in that direction I turned, pushing forward as rapidly as possible through the undergrowth.

Presently I came into a region where the trees were larger and the travelling was easier. It was not a primeval forest, but a second growth of chestnuts and poplars and maples. Through the woods there ran at intervals long lines of broken rock, covered with moss—the ruins, evidently, of ancient stone fences. The land must have been, in former days, a farm, inhabited, cultivated, the home of human

hopes and desires and labours, but now relapsed
into solitude and wilderness. What could the life
have been among these rugged and inhospitable
Highlands, on this niggard and reluctant soil?
Where was the house that once sheltered the tillers
of this rude corner of the earth?

Here, perhaps, in the little clearing into which
I now emerged. A couple of decrepit apple-trees
grew on the edge of it, and dropped their scanty
and gnarled fruit to feast the squirrels. A little
farther on, a straggling clump of ancient lilacs, a
bewildered old bush of sweetbrier, the dark-green
leaves of a cluster of tiger-lilies, long past blooming, marked the grave of the garden. And here,
above this square hollow in the earth, with the re-
mains of a crumbling chimney standing sentinel
beside it, here the house must have stood. What
joys, what sorrows once centred around this cold
and desolate hearth-stone? What children went
forth like birds from this dismantled nest into the
wide world? What guests found refuge——

"Take care! stand back! There is a rattlesnake
in the old cellar."

77

THE BLUE FLOWER

The voice, even more than the words, startled me. I drew away suddenly, and saw, behind the ruins of the chimney, a man of an aspect so striking that to this day his face and figure are as vivid in my memory as if it were but yesterday that I had met him.

He was dressed in black, the coat of a somewhat formal cut, a long cravat loosely knotted in his rolling collar. His head was bare, and the coal-black hair, thick and waving, was in some disorder. His face, smooth and pale, with high forehead, straight nose, and thin, sensitive lips—was it old or young? Handsome it certainly was, the face of a man of mark, a man of power. Yet there was something strange and wild about it. His dark eyes, with the fine wrinkles about them, had a look of unspeakable remoteness, and at the same time an intensity that seemed to pierce me through and through. It was as if he saw me in a dream, yet measured me, weighed me with a scrutiny as exact as it was at bottom indifferent.

But his lips were smiling, and there was no fault to be found, at least, with his manner. He had risen

78

from the broad stone where he had evidently been sitting with his back against the chimney, and came forward to greet me.

"You will pardon the abruptness of my greeting? I thought you might not care to make acquaintance with the present tenant of this old house—at least not without an introduction."

"Certainly not," I answered, "you have done me a real kindness, which is better than the outward form of courtesy. But how is it that you stay at such close quarters with this unpleasant tenant? Have you no fear of him?"

"Not the least in the world," he answered, laughing. "I know the snakes too well, better than they know themselves. It is not likely that even an old serpent with thirteen rattles, like this one, could harm me. I know his ways. Before he could strike I should be out of reach."

"Well," said I, "it is a grim thought, at all events, that this house, once a cheerful home, no doubt, should have fallen at last to be the dwelling of such a vile creature."

"Fallen!" he exclaimed. Then he repeated the

79

word with a questioning accent—"fallen? Are you sure of that? The snake, in his way, may be quite as honest as the people who lived here before him, and not much more harmful. The farmer was a miser who robbed his mother, quarrelled with his brother, and starved his wife. What she lacked in food, she made up in drink, when she could. One of the children, a girl, was a cripple, lamed by her mother in a fit of rage. The two boys were ne'er-do-weels who ran away from home as soon as they were old enough. One of them is serving a life-sentence in the State prison for manslaughter. When the house burned down some thirty years ago, the woman escaped. The man's body was found with the head crushed in—perhaps by a falling timber. The family of our friend the rattlesnake could hardly surpass that record, I think. But why should we blame them—any of them? They were only acting out their natures. To one who can see and understand, it is all perfectly simple, and in-teresting—immensely interesting."

It is impossible to describe the quiet eagerness, the cool glow of fervour with which he narrated this little history. It was the manner of the triumphant pathologist who lays bare some hidden seat of disease. It surprised and repelled me a little; yet it attracted me, too, for I could see how evidently he counted on my comprehension and sympathy.

"Well," said I, "it is a pitiful history. Rural life is not all peace and innocence. But how came you to know the story?"

"I? Oh, I make it my business to know a little of everything, and as much as possible of human life, not excepting the petty chronicles of the rustics around me. It is my chief pleasure. I earn my living by teaching boys. I find my satisfaction in studying men. But you are on a journey, sir, and night is falling. I must not detain you. Or perhaps you will allow me to forward you a little by serving as a guide. Which way were you going when you turned aside to look at this dismantled shrine?"

"To Canterbury," I answered, "to find a night's, or a month's, lodging at the inn. My journey is a ramble, it has neither terminus nor time-table."

"Then let me commend to you something vastly better than the tender mercies of the Canterbury Inn. Come with me to the school on Hilltop, where I am a teacher. It is a thousand feet above the village—purer air, finer view, and pleasanter company. There is plenty of room in the house, for it is vacation-time. Master Isaac Ward is always glad to entertain guests."

There was something so sudden and unconventional about the invitation that I was reluctant to accept it; but he gave it naturally and pressed it with earnest courtesy, assuring me that it was in accordance with Master Ward's custom, that he would be much disappointed to lose the chance of talking with an interesting traveller, that he would far rather let me pay him for my lodging than have me go by, and so on—so that at last I consented.

Three minutes' walking from the deserted clearing brought us into a travelled road. It circled the breast of the mountain, and as we stepped along it in the dusk I learned something of my companion. His name was Edward Keene; he taught Latin and Greek in the Hilltop School; he had studied for the ministry, but had given it up, I gathered, on account of a certain loss of interest, or rather a diversion of interest in another direction. He spoke of himself with an impersonal candour.

"Preachers must be always trying to persuade men," he said. "But what I care about is to know men. I don't care what they do. Certainly I have no wish to interfere with them in their doings, for I doubt whether anyone can really change them. Each tree bears its own fruit, you see, and by their fruits you know them."

"What do you say to grafting? That changes the fruit, surely?"

"Yes, but a grafted tree is not really one tree. It is two trees growing together. There is a double life in it, and the second life, the added life, dominates the other. The stock becomes a kind of animate soil for the graft to grow in."

Presently the road dipped into a little valley and rose again, breasting the slope of a wooded hill which thrust itself out from the steeper flank of the mountain-range. Down the hill-side a song

floated to meet us—that most noble lyric of old
Robert Herrick:

> *Bid me to live, and I will live*
> *Thy Protestant to be ;*
> *Or bid me love, and I will give*
> *A loving heart to thee.*

It was a girl's voice, fresh and clear, with a
note of tenderness in it that thrilled me. Keene's
pace quickened. And soon the singer came in sight,
stepping lightly down the road, a shape of slender
whiteness on the background of gathering night.
She was beautiful even in that dim light, with
brown eyes and hair, and a face that seemed to
breathe purity and trust. Yet there was a trace
of anxiety in it, or so I fancied, that gave it an
appealing charm.

"You have come at last, Edward," she cried,
running forward and putting her hand in his.
"It is late. You have been out all day; I began to
be afraid."

"Not too late," he answered; "there was no need
for fear, Dorothy. I am not alone, you see." And

keeping her hand, he introduced me to the daughter of Master Ward.

It was easy to guess the relation between these two young people who walked beside me in the dusk. It needed no words to say that they were lovers. Yet it would have needed many words to define the sense, that came to me gradually, of something singular in the tie that bound them together. On his part there was a certain tone of half-playful condescension toward her such as one might use to a lovely child, which seemed to match but ill with her unconscious attitude of watchful care, of tender solicitude for him—almost like the manner of an elder sister. Lovers they surely were, and acknowledged lovers, for their frankness of demeanour sought no concealment; but I felt that there must be

A little rift within the lute,

though neither of them might know it. Each one's thought of the other was different from the other's thought of self. There could not be a complete understanding, a perfect accord. What was the secret, of which each knew half, but not the other half?

Thus, with steps that kept time, but with thoughts how wide apart, we came to the door of the school. A warm flood of light poured out to greet us. The Master, an elderly, placid, comfortable man, gave me just the welcome that had been promised in his name. The supper was waiting, and the evening passed in such happy cheer that the bewilderments and misgivings of the twilight melted away, and at bedtime I dropped into the nest of sleep as one who has found a shelter among friends.

II

THE Hilltop School stood on a blessed site. Lifted high above the village, it held the crest of the last gentle wave of the mountains that filled the south with crowding billows, ragged and tumultuous. Northward, the great plain lay at our feet, smiling in the sun; meadows and groves, yellow fields of harvest and green orchards, white roads and clustering towns, with here and there a little city on the bank of the mighty river which curved in a vast line of beauty toward the blue Catskill Range, fifty miles away. Lines of filmy smoke, like vanishing footprints in the air, marked the passage of railway trains across the landscape—their swift flight reduced by distance to a leisurely transition. The bright surface of the stream was furrowed by a hundred vessels; tiny rowboats creeping from shore to shore; knots of black barges following the lead of puffing tugs; sloops with languid motion tacking against the tide; white steamboats, like huge toy-houses, crowded with pygmy inhabitants, moving smoothly on their way to the great city, and disappearing suddenly as they turned into the narrows between Storm-King and the Fishkill Mountains. Down there was life, incessant, varied, restless, intricate, many-coloured —down there was history, the highway of ancient voyagers since the days of Hendrik Hudson, the hunting-ground of Indian tribes, the scenes of massacre and battle, the last camp of the Army of the Revolution, the Head-quarters of Washington—down there were the homes of legend and

87

poetry, the dreamlike hills of Rip van Winkle's sleep, the cliffs and caves haunted by the Culprit Fay, the solitudes traversed by the Spy—all outspread before us, and visible as in a Claude Lorraine glass, in the tranquil lucidity of distance. And here, on the hilltop, was our own life; secluded, yet never separated from the other life; looking down upon it, yet woven of the same stuff; peaceful in circumstance, yet ever busy with its own tasks, and holding in its quiet heart all the elements of joy and sorrow and tragic consequence.

The Master was a man of most unworldly wisdom. In his youth a great traveller, he had brought home many observations, a few views, and at least one theory. To him the school was the most important of human institutions—more vital even than the home, because it held the first real experience of social contact, of free intercourse with other minds and lives coming from different households and embodying different strains of blood. "My school," said he, "is the world in miniature. If I can teach these boys to study and play together freely and with fairness to one another, I shall make men fit to live and work together in society. What they learn matters less than how they learn it. The great thing is the bringing out of individual character so that it will find its place in social harmony."

Yet never man knew less of character in the concrete than Master Ward. To him each person represented a type—the scientific, the practical, the poetic. From each one he expected, and in each one he found, to a certain degree, the fruit of the marked quality, the obvious, the characteristic. But of the deeper character, made up of a hundred traits, coloured and conditioned most vitally by something secret and in itself apparently of slight importance, he was placidly unconscious. Classes he knew. Individuals escaped him. Yet he was a most companionable man, a social solitary, a friendly hermit.

His daughter Dorothy seemed to me even more fair and appealing by daylight than when I first saw her in the dusk. There was a pure brightness in her brown eyes, a gentle dignity in her look

and bearing, a soft cadence of expectant joy in
her voice. She was womanly in every tone and motion, yet by no means weak or uncertain. Mistress
of herself and of the house, she ruled her kingdom
without an effort. Busied with many little cares,
she bore them lightly. Her spirit overflowed into
the lives around her with delicate sympathy and
merry cheer. But it was in music that her nature
found its widest outlet. In the lengthening evenings of late August she would play from Schu-
mann, or Chopin, or Grieg, interpreting the vague
feelings of gladness or grief which lie too deep for
words. Ballads she loved, quaint old English and
Scotch airs, folk-songs of Germany, "Come-all-
ye's" of Ireland, Canadian *chansons*. She sang—
not like an angel, but like a woman.

Of the two under-masters in the school, Edward
Keene was the elder. The younger, John Graham,
was his opposite in every respect. Sturdy, fair-
haired, plain in the face, he was essentially an
every-day man, devoted to out-of-door sports, a
hard worker, a good player, and a sound sleeper.
He came back to the school, from a fishing-excur-

sion, a few days after my arrival. I liked the way in which he told of his adventures, with a little frank boasting, enough to season but not to spoil the story. I liked the way in which he took hold of his work, helping to get the school in readiness for the return of the boys in the middle of September. I liked, more than all, his attitude to Dorothy Ward. He loved her, clearly enough. When she was in the room the other people were only accidents to him. Yet there was nothing of the disappointed suitor in his bearing. He was cheerful, natural, accepting the situation, giving her the best he had to give, and gladly taking from her the frank reliance, the ready comradeship which she bestowed upon him. If he envied Keene—and how could he help it—at least he never showed a touch of jealousy or rivalry. The engagement was a fact which he took into account as something not to be changed or questioned. Keene was so much more brilliant, interesting, attractive. He answered so much more fully to the poetic side of Dorothy's nature. How could she help preferring him?

Thus the three actors in the drama stood, when

I became an inmate of Hilltop, and accepted the master's invitation to undertake some of the minor classes in English, and stay on at the school indefinitely. It was my wish to see the little play—a pleasant comedy, I hoped—move forward to a happy ending. And yet—what was it that disturbed me now and then with forebodings? Something, doubtless, in the character of Keene, for he was the dominant personality. The key of the situation lay with him. He was the centre of interest. Yet he was the one who seemed not perfectly in harmony, not quite at home, as if something beckoned and urged him away.

"I am glad you are to stay," said he, "yet I wonder at it. You will find the life narrow, after all your travels. Ulysses at Ithaca—you will surely be restless to see the world again."

"If you find the life broad enough, I ought not to be cramped in it."

" Ah, but I have compensations."

"One you certainly have," said I, thinking of Dorothy, "and that one is enough to make a man happy anywhere."

"Yes, yes," he answered, quickly, "but that is not what I mean. It is not there that I look for a wider life. Love—do you think that love broadens a man's outlook? To me it seems to make him narrower—happier, perhaps, within his own little circle—but distinctly narrower. Knowledge is the only thing that broadens life, sets it free from the tyranny of the parish, fills it with the sense of power. And love is the opposite of knowledge. Love is a kind of an illusion—a happy illusion, that is what love is. Don't you see that?"

"See it?" I cried. "I don't know what you mean. Do you mean that you don't really care for Dorothy Ward? Do you mean that what you have won in her is an illusion? If so, you are as wrong as a man can be."

"No, no," he answered, eagerly, "you know I don't mean that. I could not live without her. But love is not the only reality. There is something else, something broader, something——"

"Come away," I said, "come away, man! You are talking nonsense, treason. You are not true to yourself. You've been working too hard at your books. There's a maggot in your brain. Come out for a long walk."

That indeed was what he liked best. He was a magnificent walker, easy, steady, unwearying. He knew every road and lane in the valleys, every footpath and trail among the mountains. But he cared little for walking in company; one companion was the most that he could abide. And, strange to say, it was not Dorothy whom he chose for his most frequent comrade. With her he would saunter down the Black Brook path, or climb slowly to the first ridge of Storm-King. But with me he pushed out to the farthest pinnacle that overhangs the river, and down through the Lonely Heart gorge, and over the pass of the White Horse, and up to the peak of Cro' Nest, and across the rugged summit of Black Rock. At every wider outlook a strange exhilaration seemed to come upon him. His spirit glowed like a live coal in the wind. He overflowed with brilliant talk and curious stories of the villages and scattered houses that we could see from our eyries.

But it was not with me that he made his longest

expeditions. They were solitary. Early on Saturday he would leave the rest of us, with some slight excuse, and start away on the mountain-road, to be gone all day. Sometimes he would not return till long after dark. Then I could see the anxious look deepen on Dorothy's face, and she would slip away down the road to meet him. But he always came back in good spirits, talkable and charming. It was the next day that the reaction came. The black fit took him. He was silent, moody, bitter. Holding himself aloof, yet never giving utterance to any irritation, he seemed half-unconsciously to resent the claims of love and friendship, as if they irked him. There was a look in his eyes as if he measured us, weighed us, analysed us all as strangers.

Yes, even Dorothy. I have seen her go to meet him with a flower in her hand that she had plucked for him, and turn away with her lips trembling, too proud to say a word, dropping the flower on the grass. John Graham saw it, too. He waited till she was gone; then he picked up the flower and kept it.

There was nothing to take offence at, nothing on which one could lay a finger; only these singular alternations of mood which made Keene now the most delightful of friends, now an intimate stranger in the circle. The change was inexplicable. But certainly it seemed to have some connection, as cause or consequence, with his long, lonely walks.

Once, when he was absent, we spoke of his remarkable fluctuations of spirit.

The master labelled him. "He is an idealist, a dreamer. They are always uncertain."

I blamed him. "He gives way too much to his moods. He lacks self-control. He is in danger of spoiling a fine nature."

I looked at Dorothy. She defended him. "Why should he be always the same? He is too great for that. His thoughts make him restless, and sometimes he is tired. Surely you wouldn't have him act what he don't feel. Why do you want him to do that?"

"I don't know," said Graham, with a short laugh. "None of us know. But what we all want

just now is music. Dorothy, will you sing a little
for us?"

So she sang "The Coulin," and "The Days o'
the Kerry Dancin'," and "The Hawthorn Tree,"
and "The Green Woods of Truigha," and "Flowers o' the Forest," and "*A la claire Fontaine*,"
until the twilight was filled with peace.

The boys came back to the school. The wheels
of routine began to turn again, slowly and with a
little friction at first, then smoothly and swiftly
as if they had never stopped. Summer reddened
into autumn; autumn bronzed into fall. The maples and poplars were bare. The oaks alone kept
their rusted crimson glory, and the cloaks of
spruce and hemlock on the shoulders of the hills
grew dark with wintry foliage. Keene's transitions
of mood became more frequent and more extreme.
The gulf of isolation that divided him from us
when the black days came seemed wider and more
unfathomable. Dorothy and John Graham were
thrown more constantly together. Keene appeared
to encourage their companionship. He watched
them curiously, sometimes, not as if he were jeal-

ous, but rather as if he were interested in some delicate experiment. At other times he would be singularly indifferent to everything, remote, abstracted, forgetful.

Dorothy's birthday, which fell in mid-October, was kept as a holiday. In the morning everyone had some little birthday gift for her, except Keene. He had forgotten the birthday entirely. The shadow of disappointment that quenched the brightness of her face was pitiful. Even he could not be blind to it. He flushed as if surprised, and hesitated a moment, evidently in conflict with himself. Then a look of shame and regret came into his eyes. He made some excuse for not going with us to the picnic, at the Black Brook Falls, with which the day was celebrated. In the afternoon, as we all sat around the camp-fire, he came swinging through the woods with his long, swift stride, and going at once to Dorothy laid a little brooch of pearl and opal in her hand.

"Will you forgive me?" he said. "I hope this is not too late. But I lost the train back from Newburg and walked home. I pray that you may

98

never know any tears but pearls, and that there may be nothing changeable about you but the opal."

"Oh, Edward!" she cried, "how beautiful! Thank you a thousand times. But I wish you had been with us all day. We have missed you so much!"

For the rest of that day simplicity and clearness and joy came back to us. Keene was at his best, a leader of friendly merriment, a master of good-fellowship, a prince of delicate chivalry. Dorothy's loveliness unfolded like a flower in the sun.

But the Indian summer of peace was brief. It was hardly a week before Keene's old moods returned, darker and stranger than ever. The girl's unconcealable bewilderment, her sense of wounded loyalty and baffled anxiety, her still look of hurt and wondering tenderness, increased from day to day. John Graham's temper seemed to change, suddenly and completely. From the best-humoured and most careless fellow in the world, he became silent, thoughtful, irritable toward everyone except

99

Dorothy. With Keene he was curt and impatient, avoiding him as much as possible, and when they were together, evidently struggling to keep down a deep dislike and rising anger. They had had sharp words when they were alone, I was sure, but Keene's coolness seemed to grow with Graham's heat. There was no open quarrel.

One Saturday evening, Graham came to me. "You have seen what is going on here?" he said.

"Something, at least," I answered, "and I am very sorry for it. But I don't quite understand it."

"Well, I do; and I'm going to put an end to it. I'm going to have it out with Ned Keene. He is breaking her heart."

"But are you the right one to take the matter up?"

"Who else is there to do it?"

"Her father."

"He sees nothing, comprehends nothing. 'Practical type—poetic type—misunderstandings sure to arise—come together after a while—each supply the other's deficiencies.' Cursed folly! And the girl is so unhappy that she can't tell anyone. It shall not go on, I say. Keene is out on the road now, taking one of his infernal walks. I'm going to meet him."

"I'm afraid it will make trouble. Let me go with you."

"The trouble is made. Come if you like. I'm going now."

The night lay heavy upon the forest. Where the road dipped through the valley we could hardly see a rod ahead of us. But higher up where the way curved around the breast of the mountain, the woods were thin on the left, and on the right a sheer precipice fell away to the gorge of the brook. In the dim starlight we saw Keene striding toward us. Graham stepped out to meet him.

"Where have you been, Ned Keene?" he cried. The cry was a challenge. Keene lifted his head and stood still. Then he laughed and took a step forward.

"Taking a long walk, Jack Graham," he answered. "It was glorious. You should have been with me. But why this sudden question?"

"Because your long walk is a pretence. You are

playing false. There is some woman that you go to see at West Point, at Highland Falls, who knows where?"

Keene laughed again.

"Certainly you don't know, my dear fellow; and neither do I. Since when has walking become a vice in your estimation? You seem to be in a fierce mood. What's the matter?"

"I will tell you what's the matter. You have been acting like a brute to the girl you profess to love."

"Plain words! But between friends frankness is best. Did she ask you to tell me?"

"No! You know too well she would die before she would speak. You are killing her, that is what you are doing with your devilish moods and mysteries. You must stop. Do you hear? You must give her up."

"I hear well enough, and it sounds like a word for her and two for yourself. Is that it?"

"Damn you," cried the younger man, "let the words go! we'll settle it this way"——and he sprang at the other's throat.

Keene, cool and well-braced, met him with a heavy blow in the chest. He recoiled, and I rushed between them, holding Graham back, and pleading for self-control. As we stood thus, panting and confused, on the edge of the cliff, a singing voice floated up to us from the shadows across the valley. It was Herrick's song again:

> *A heart as soft, a heart as kind,*
> *A heart as sound and free*
> *As in the whole world thou canst find,*
> *That heart I'll give to thee.*

"Come, gentlemen," I cried, "this is folly, sheer madness. You can never deal with the matter in this way. Think of the girl who is singing down yonder. What would happen to her, what would she suffer, from scandal, from her own feelings, if either of you should be killed, or even seriously hurt by the other? There must be no quarrel between you."

"Certainly," said Keene, whose poise, if shaken at all, had returned, "certainly, you are right. It is not of my seeking, nor shall I be the one to keep it up. I am willing to let it pass. It is but a small matter at most."

I turned to Graham—"And you?"

He hesitated a little, and then said, doggedly: "On one condition."

"And that is?"

"Keene must explain. He must answer my question."

"Do you accept?" I asked Keene.

"Yes and no!" he replied. "No! to answering Graham's question. He is not the person to ask it. I wonder that he does not see the impropriety, the absurdity of his meddling at all in this affair. Besides, he could not understand my answer even if he believed it. But to the explanation, I say, Yes! I will give it, not to Graham, but to you. I make you this proposition. To-morrow is Sunday. We shall be excused from service if we tell the master that we have important business to settle together. You shall come with me on one of my long walks. I will tell you all about them. Then you can be the judge whether there is any harm in them."

"Does that satisfy you?" I said to Graham.

"Yes," he answered, "that seems fair enough. I am content to leave it in that way for the present. And to make it still more fair, I want to take back what I said awhile ago, and to ask Keene's pardon for it."

"Not at all," said Keene, quickly, "it was said in haste, I bear no grudge. You simply did not understand, that is all."

So we turned to go down the hill, and as we turned, Dorothy met us, coming out of the shadows.

"What are you men doing here?" she asked. "I heard your voices from below. What were you talking about?"

"We were talking," said Keene, "my dear Dorothy, we were talking—about walking—yes, that was it—about walking, and about views. The conversation was quite warm, almost a debate. Now, you know all the view-points in this region. Which do you call the best, the most satisfying, the finest prospect? But I know what you will say: the view from the little knoll in front of Hilltop. For there, when you are tired of looking far away, you can turn around and see the old school, and the linden-trees, and the garden."

"Yes," she answered gravely, "that is really the view that I love best. I would give up all the others rather than lose that."

III

THERE was a softness in the November air that brought back memories of summer, and a few be-lated daisies were blooming in the old clearing, as Keene and I passed by the ruins of the farm-house again, early on Sunday morning. He had been talking ever since we started, pouring out his praise of knowledge, wide, clear, universal knowl-edge, as the best of life's joys, the greatest of life's achievements. The practical life was a blind, dull routine. Most men were toiling at tasks which they did not like, by rules which they did not under-stand. They never looked beyond the edge of their work. The philosophical life was a spider's web—filmy threads of theory spun out of the inner consciousness—it touched the world only at certain chosen points of attachment. There was nothing firm, nothing substantial in it. You could look through it like a veil and see the real world lying beyond. But the theorist could see only the web which he had spun. Knowing did not come by speculating, theorising. Knowing came by seeing. Vision was the only real knowledge. To see the world, the whole world, as it is, to look behind the scenes, to read human life like a book, that was the glorious thing—most satisfying, divine.

Thus he had talked as we climbed the hill. Now, as we came by the place where we had first met, a new eagerness sounded in his voice.

"Ever since that day I have inclined to tell you something more about myself. I felt sure you would understand. I am planning to write a book— a book of knowledge, in the true sense—a great book about human life. Not a history, not a theory, but a real view of life, its hidden motives, its secret relations. How different they are from what men dream and imagine and play that they are! How much darker, how much smaller, and therefore how much more interesting and wonderful. No one has yet written—perhaps because no one has yet conceived—such a book as I have in mind. I might call it a 'Bionopsis.' "

"But surely," said I, "you have chosen a strange place to write it—the Hilltop School—this quiet and secluded region! The stream of humanity is very slow and slender here—it trickles. You must get out into the busy world. You must be in the full current and feel its force. You must take part in the active life of mankind in order really to know it."

"A mistake!" he cried. "Action is the thing that blinds men. You remember Matthew Arnold's line:

In action's dizzying eddy whirled.

To know the world you must stand apart from it and above it; you must look down on it."

"Well, then," said I, "you will have to find some secret spring of inspiration, some point of vantage from which you can get your outlook and your insight."

He stopped short and looked me full in the face.

"And that," cried he, "is precisely what I have found!"

Then he turned and pushed along the narrow trail so swiftly that I had hard work to follow him. After a few minutes we came to a little stream, flowing through a grove of hemlocks. Keene seated himself on the fallen log that served for a bridge and beckoned me to a place beside him.

"I promised to give you an explanation to-day —to take you on one of my long walks. Well, there is only one of them. It is always the same. You shall see where it leads, what it means. You shall share my secret—all the wonder and glory of it! Of course I know my conduct has seemed strange to you. Sometimes it has seemed strange even to me. I have been doubtful, troubled, almost distracted. I have been risking a great deal, in danger of losing what I value, what most men count the best thing in the world. But it could not be helped. The risk was worth while. A great discovery, the opportunity of a lifetime, yes, of an age, perhaps of many ages, came to me. I simply could not throw it away. I must use it, make the best of it,

109

at any danger, at any cost. You shall judge for yourself whether I was right or wrong. But you must judge fairly, without haste, without prejudice. I ask you to make me one promise. You will suspend judgment, you will say nothing, you will keep my secret, until you have been with me three times at the place where I am now taking you."

By this time it was clear to me that I had to do with a case lying far outside of the common routine of life; something subtle, abnormal, hard to measure, in which a clear and careful estimate would be necessary. If Keene was labouring under some strange delusion, some disorder of mind, how could I estimate its nature or extent, without time and study, perhaps without expert advice? To wait a little would be prudent, for his sake as well as for the sake of others. If there was some extraordinary reality behind his mysterious hints, it would need patience and skill to test it. I gave him the promise for which he asked.

At once, as if relieved, he sprang up, and crying, "Come on, follow me!" began to make his way up the bed of the brook. It was one of the wildest

walks that I have ever taken. He turned aside for
no obstacles; swamps, masses of interlacing alders,
close-woven thickets of stiff young spruces,
chevaux-de-frise of dead trees where wind-falls had
mowed down the forest, walls of lichen-crusted
rock, landslides where heaps of broken stone were
tumbled in ruinous confusion—through everything he pushed forward. I could see, here and
there, the track of his former journeys: broken
branches of witch-hazel and moose-wood, ferns
trampled down, a faint trail across some deeper
bed of moss. At mid-day we rested for a half-hour
to eat lunch. But Keene would eat nothing, except
a little pellet of some dark green substance that he
took from a flat silver box in his pocket. He swal-
lowed it hastily, and stooping his face to the
spring by which he had halted, drank long and
eagerly.

"An Indian trick," said he, shaking the drops
of water from his face. "On a walk, food is a hindrance, a delay. But this tiny taste of bitter gum
is a tonic; it spurs the courage and doubles the
strength—if you are used to it. Otherwise I should

not recommend you to try it. Faugh! the flavour is vile."

He rinsed his mouth again with water, and stood up, calling me to come on. The way, now tangled among the nameless peaks and ranges, bore steadily southward, rising all the time, in spite of many brief downward curves where a steep gorge must be crossed. Presently we came into a hard-wood forest, open and easy to travel. Breasting a long slope, we reached the summit of a broad, smoothly rounding ridge covered with a dense growth of stunted spruce. The trees rose above our heads, about twice the height of a man, and so thick that we could not see beyond them. But, from glimpses here and there, and from the purity and lightness of the air, I judged that we were on far higher ground than any we had yet traversed, the central comb, perhaps, of the mountain-system.

A few yards ahead of us, through the crowded trunks of the dwarf forest, I saw a gray mass, like the wall of a fortress, across our path. It was a vast rock, rising from the crest of the ridge, lifting its top above the sea of foliage. At its base there were heaps of shattered stones, and deep crevices almost like caves. One side of the rock was broken by a slanting gully.

"Be careful," cried my companion, "there is a rattlers' den somewhere about here. The snakes are in their winter quarters now, almost dormant, but they can still strike if you tread on them. Step here! Give me your hand—use that point of rock— hold fast by this bush; it is firmly rooted—so! Here we are on Spy Rock! You have heard of it? I thought so. Other people have heard of it, and imagine that they have found it—five miles east of us—on a lower ridge. Others think it is a peak just back of Cro' Nest. All wrong! There is but one real Spy Rock—here! This earth holds no more perfect view-point. It is one of the rare places from which a man may see the kingdoms of the world and all the glory of them. Look!"

The prospect was indeed magnificent; it was strange what a vast enlargement of vision resulted from the slight elevation above the surrounding peaks. It was like being lifted up so that we could look over the walls. The horizon expanded as if by magic. The vast circumference of vision swept around us with a radius of a hundred miles. Mountain and meadow, forest and field, river and lake, hill and dale, village and farmland, far-off city and shimmering water—all lay open to our sight, and over all the westering sun wove a transparent robe of gem-like hues. Every feature of the landscape seemed alive, quivering, pulsating with conscious beauty. You could almost see the world breathe.

"Wonderful!" I cried. "Most wonderful! You have found a mount of vision."

"Ah," he answered, "you don't half see the wonder yet, you don't begin to appreciate it. Your eyes are new to it. You have not learned the power of far sight, the secret of Spy Rock. You are still shut in by the horizon."

"Do you mean to say that you can look beyond it?"

"Beyond yours—yes. And beyond any that you would dream possible—See! Your sight reaches to that dim cloud of smoke in the south? And beneath it you can make out, perhaps, a vague blotch of shadow, or a tiny flash of brightness where the sun strikes it? New York! But I can see the great buildings, the domes, the spires, the crowded wharves, the tides of people whirling through the streets—and beyond that, the sea, with the ships coming and going! I can follow them on their courses—and beyond that—Oh! when I am on Spy Rock I can see more than other men can imagine."

For a moment, strange to say, I almost fancied I could follow him. The magnetism of his spirit imposed upon me, carried me away with him. Then sober reason told me that he was talking of impossibilities.

"Keene," said I, "you are dreaming. The view and the air have intoxicated you. This is a phantasy, a delusion!"

"It pleases you to call it so," he said, "but I only tell you my real experience. Why it should be impossible I do not understand. There is no reason why the power of sight should not be cultivated, enlarged, expanded indefinitely."

"And the straight rays of light?" I asked.

"And the curvature of the earth which makes a horizon inevitable?"

"Who knows what a ray of light is?" said he. "Who can prove that it may not be curved, under certain conditions, or refracted in some places in a way that is not possible elsewhere? I tell you there is something extraordinary about this Spy Rock. It is a seat of power—Nature's observatory. More things are visible here than anywhere else— more than I have told you yet. But come, we have little time left. For half an hour, each of us shall enjoy what he can see. Then home again to the narrower outlook, the restricted life."

The downward journey was swifter than the ascent, but no less fatiguing. By the time we reached the school, an hour after dark, I was very tired. But Keene was in one of his moods of exhilaration. He glowed like a piece of phosphorus that has been drenched with light.

Graham took the first opportunity of speaking with me alone.

"Well?" said he.

"Well!" I answered. "You were wrong. There

116

is no treason in Keene's walks, no guilt in his
moods. But there is something very strange. I cannot form a judgment yet as to what we should do.
We must wait a few days. It will do no harm to
be patient. Indeed, I have promised not to judge,
not to speak of it, until a certain time. Are you
satisfied?"

"This is a curious story," said he, "and I am
puzzled by it. But I trust you, I agree to wait,
though I am far from satisfied."

Our second expedition was appointed for the
following Saturday. Keene was hungry for it, and
I was almost as eager, desiring to penetrate as
quickly as possible into the heart of the affair.
Already a conviction in regard to it was pressing
upon me, and I resolved to let him talk, this time,
as freely as he would, without interruption or
denial.

When we clambered up on Spy Rock, he was
more subdued and reserved than he had been the
first time. For a while he talked little, but scanned
the view with wide, shining eyes. Then he began

to tell me stories of the places that we could see—strange stories of domestic calamity, and social conflict, and eccentric passion, and hidden crime.

"Do you remember Hawthorne's story of 'The Minister's Black Veil?' It is the best comment on human life that ever was written. Everyone has something to hide. The surface of life is a mask. The substance of life is a secret. All humanity wears the black veil. But it is not impenetrable. No, it is transparent, if you find the right point of view. Here, on Spy Rock, I have found it. I have learned how to look through the veil. I can see, not by the light-rays only, but by the rays which are colourless, imperceptible, irresistible—the rays of the unknown quantity, which penetrate everywhere. I can see how men down in the great city are weaving their nets of selfishness and falsehood, and calling them industrial enterprises or political combinations. I can see how the wheels of society are moved by the hidden springs of avarice and greed and rivalry. I can see how children drink in the fables of religion, without understanding them, and how prudent men repeat them without

118

believing them. I can see how the illusions of love appear and vanish, and how men and women swear that their dreams are eternal, even while they fade. I can see how poor people blind themselves and deceive each other, calling selfishness devotion, and bondage contentment. Down at Hilltop yonder I can see how Dorothy Ward and John Graham, without knowing it, without meaning it——"

"Stop, man!" I cried. "Stop, before you say what can never be unsaid. You know it is not true. These are nightmare visions that ride you. Not from Spy Rock nor from anywhere else can you see anything at Hilltop that is not honest and pure and loyal. Come down, now, and let us go home. You will see better there than here."

"I think not," said he, "but I will come. Yes, of course, I am bound to come. But let me have a few minutes here alone. Go you down along the path a little way slowly. I will follow you in a quarter of an hour. And remember we are to be here together once more!"

Once more! Yes, and then what must be done?

How was this strange case to be dealt with so as to save all the actors, as far as possible, from needless suffering? That Keene's mind was disordered at least three of us suspected already. But to me alone was the nature and seat of the disorder known. How make the others understand it? They might easily conceive it to be something different from the fact, some actual lesion of the brain, an incurable insanity. But this it was not. As yet, at least, he was no patient for a mad-house: it would be unjust, probably it would be impossible to have him committed. But on the other hand they might take it too lightly, as the result of overwork, or perhaps of the use of some narcotic. To me it was certain that the trouble went far deeper than this. It lay in the man's moral nature, in the error of his central will. It was the working out, in abnormal form, but with essential truth, of his chosen and cherished ideal of life. Spy Rock was something more than the seat of his delusion. It was the expression of his temperament. The solitary trail that led thither was the symbol of his search for happiness—alone, forgetful of life's lowlier ties, looking down upon the world in the cold abstraction of scornful knowledge. How was such a man to be brought back to the real life whose first condition is the acceptance of a limited out-look, the willingness to live by trust as much as by sight, the power of finding joy and peace in the things that we feel are the best, even though we cannot prove them nor explain them? How could he ever bring anything but discord and sor-row to those who were bound to him?

This was what perplexed and oppressed me. I needed all the time until the next Saturday to think the question through, to decide what should be done. But the matter was taken out of my hands. After our latest expedition Keene's dark mood re-turned upon him with sombre intensity. Dull, rest-less, indifferent, half-contemptuous, he seemed to withdraw into himself, observing those around him with half-veiled glances, as if he had nothing better to do and yet found it a tiresome pastime. He was like a man waiting wearily at a railway station for his train. Nothing pleased him. He responded to nothing.

Graham controlled his indignation by a constant effort. A dozen times he was on the point of speaking out. But he restrained himself and played fair. Dorothy's suffering could not be hidden. Her loyalty was strained to the breaking point. She was too tender and true for anger, but she was wounded almost beyond endurance.

Keene's restlessness increased. The intervening Thursday was Thanksgiving Day; most of the boys had gone home; the school had holiday. Early in the morning he came to me.

"Let us take our walk to-day. We have no work to do. Come! In this clear, frosty air, Spy Rock will be glorious!"

"No," I answered, "this is no day for such an expedition. This is the home day. Stay here and be happy with us all. You owe this to love and friendship. You owe it to Dorothy Ward."

"Owe it?" said he. "Speaking of debts, I think each man is his own preferred creditor. But of course you can do as you like about to-day. To-morrow or Saturday will answer just as well for our third walk together."

About noon he came down from his room and went to the piano, where Dorothy was sitting. They talked together in low tones. Then she stood up, with pale face and wide-open eyes. She laid her hand on his arm.

"Do not go, Edward. For the last time I beg you to stay with us to-day."

He lifted her hand and held it for an instant. Then he bowed, and let it fall.

"You will excuse me, Dorothy, I am sure. I feel the need of exercise. Absolutely I must go; good-by—until the evening."

The hours of that day passed heavily for all of us. There was a sense of disaster in the air. Something irretrievable had fallen from our circle. But no one dared to name it. Night closed in upon the house with a changing sky. All the stars were hidden. The wind whimpered and then shouted. The rain swept down in spiteful volleys, deepening at last into a fierce, steady discharge. Nine o'clock, ten o'clock passed, and Keene did not return. By midnight we were certain that some accident had befallen him.

It was impossible to go up into the mountains in that pitch-darkness of furious tempest. But we could send down to the village for men to organise a search-party and to bring the doctor. At daybreak we set out—some of the men going with the Master along Black Brook, others in different directions to make sure of a complete search—Graham and the doctor and I following the secret trail that I knew only too well. Dorothy insisted that she must go. She would hear no denial, declaring that it would be worse for her alone at home, than if we took her with us.

It was incredible how the path seemed to lengthen. Graham watched the girl's every step, helping her over the difficult places, pushing aside the tangled branches, his eyes resting upon her as frankly, as tenderly as a mother looks at her child. In single file we marched through the gray morning, clearing cold after the storm, and the silence was seldom broken, for we had little heart to talk.

At last we came to the high, lonely ridge, the dwarf forest, the huge, couchant bulk of Spy

Rock. There, on the back of it, with his right arm hanging over the edge, was the outline of Edward Keene's form. It was as if some monster had seized him and flung him over its shoulder to carry away.

We called to him but there was no answer. The doctor climbed up with me, and we hurried to the spot where he was lying. His face was turned to the sky, his eyes blindly staring; there was no pulse, no breath; he was already cold in death. His right hand and arm, the side of his neck and face were horribly swollen and livid. The doctor stooped down and examined the hand carefully. "See!" he cried, pointing to a great bruise on his wrist, with two tiny punctures in the middle of it from which a few drops of blood had oozed, "a rattlesnake has struck him. He must have fairly put his hand upon it, perhaps in the dark, when he was climbing. And look, what is this?"

He picked up a flat silver box, that lay open on the rock. There were two olive-green pellets of a resinous paste in it. He lifted it to his face, and drew a long breath.

"Yes," he said, "it is Gunjah, the most powerful form of Hashish, the narcotic hemp of India. Poor fellow, it saved him from frightful agony. He died in a dream."

"You are right," I said, "in a dream, and for a dream."

We covered his face and climbed down the rock. Dorothy and Graham were waiting below. He had put his coat around her. She was shivering a little. There were tear-marks on her face.

"Well," I said, "you must know it. We have lost him."

"Ah!" said the girl, "I lost him long ago."

WOOD-MAGIC

WOOD-MAGIC

THERE are three vines that belong to the ancient forest. Elsewhere they will not grow, though the soil prepared for them be never so rich, the shade of the arbour built for them never so closely and cunningly woven. Their delicate, thread-like roots take no hold upon the earth tilled and troubled by the fingers of man. The fine sap that steals through their long, slender limbs pauses and fails when they are watered by human hands. Silently the secret of their life retreats and shrinks away and hides itself.

But in the woods, where falling leaves and crumbling tree-trunks and wilting ferns have been moulded by Nature into a deep, brown humus, clean and fragrant—in the woods, where the sunlight filters green and golden through interlacing branches, and where pure moisture of distilling rains and melting snows is held in treasury by never-failing banks of moss—under the verdurous flood of the forest, like sea-weeds under the ocean-waves, these three little creeping vines put forth their hands with joy, and spread over rock and hillock and twisted tree-root and mouldering log, in cloaks and scarves and wreaths of tiny ever-green, glossy leaves.

One of them is adorned with white pearls sprinkled lightly over its robe of green. This is Snowberry, and if you eat of it, you will grow wise in the wisdom of flowers. You will know where to find the yellow violet, and the wake-robin, and the pink lady-slipper, and the scarlet sage, and the fringed gentian. You will understand how the buds trust themselves to the spring in their unfold-ing, and how the blossoms trust themselves to the winter in their withering, and how the busy hands of Nature are ever weaving the beautiful garment of life out of the strands of death, and nothing is lost that yields itself to her quiet handling.

Another of the vines of the forest is called Par-tridge-berry. Rubies are hidden among its foliage, and if you eat of this fruit, you will grow wise in the wisdom of birds. You will know where the oven-bird secretes her nest, and where the woodcock dances in the air at night; the drumming-log of the ruffed grouse will be easy to find, and you will see the dark lodges of the evergreen thickets inhabited by hundreds of warblers. There will be no dead silence for you in the forest, any longer, but you will hear sweet and delicate voices on every side, voices that you know and love; you will catch the key-note of the silver flute of the wood-thrush, and the silver harp of the veery, and the silver bells of the hermit; and something in your heart will answer to them all. In the frosty stillness of October nights you will see the airy tribes flitting across the moon, following the secret call that guides them southward. In the calm brightness of winter sunshine, filling sheltered copses with warmth and cheer, you will watch the lingering blue-birds and robins and song-sparrows playing at summer, while the chick-a-dees and the juncos and the cross-bills make merry in the wind-swept fields. In the lucent mornings of April you will hear your old friends coming home to you, Phœbe, and Oriole, and Yellow-Throat, and Red-Wing, and Tanager, and Cat-Bird. When they call

to you and greet you, you will understand that
Nature knows a secret for which man has never
found a word—the secret that tells itself in song.

The third of the forest-vines is Wood-Magic.
It bears neither flower nor fruit. Its leaves are
hardly to be distinguished from the leaves of the
other vines. Perhaps they are a little rounder than
the Snowberry's, a little more pointed than the
Partridge-berry's; sometimes you might mistake
them for the one, sometimes for the other. No
marks of warning have been written upon them.
If you find them it is your fortune; if you taste
them it is your fate.

For as you browse your way through the forest,
nipping here and there a rosy leaf of young win-
ter-green, a fragrant emerald tip of balsam-fir, a
twig of spicy birch, if by chance you pluck the
leaves of Wood-Magic and eat them, you will not
know what you have done, but the enchantment of
the tree-land will enter your heart and the charm
of the wildwood will flow through your veins.

You will never get away from it. The sighing of
the wind through the pine-trees and the laughter

of the stream in its rapids will sound through all your dreams. On beds of silken softness you will long for the sleep-song of whispering leaves above your head, and the smell of a couch of balsam-boughs. At tables spread with dainty fare you will be hungry for the joy of the hunt, and for the angler's sylvan feast. In proud cities you will weary for the sight of a mountain trail; in great cathedrals you will think of the long, arching aisles of the woodland; and in the noisy solitude of crowded streets you will hone after the friendly forest.

This is what will happen to you if you eat the leaves of that little vine, Wood-Magic. And this is what happened to Luke Dubois.

I

The Cabin by the Rivers

Two highways meet before the door, and a third reaches away to the southward, broad and smooth and white. But there are no travellers passing by. The snow that has fallen during the night is unbroken. The pale February sunrise makes blue shadows on it, sharp and jagged, an outline of the fir-trees on the mountain-crest quarter of a mile away.

In summer the highways are dissolved into three wild rivers—the River of Rocks, which issues from the hills; the River of Meadows, which flows from the great lake; and the River of the Way Out, which runs down from their meeting-place to the settlements and the little world. But in winter, when the ice is firm under the snow, and the going is fine, there are no tracks upon the three broad roads except the paths of the caribou, and the footprints of the marten and the mink and the fox, and the narrow trails made by Luke Dubois on his way to and from his cabin by the rivers.

He leaned in the door-way, looking out. Behind him in the shadow, the fire was still snapping in the little stove where he had cooked his breakfast. There was a comforting smell of bacon and venison in the room; the tea-pot stood on the table half-empty. Here in the corner were his rifle and some of his traps. On the wall hung his snowshoes.

Under the bunk was a pile of skins. Half-open on the bench lay the book that he had been reading the evening before, while the snow was falling. It was a book of veritable fairy-tales, which told how men had made their way in the world, and achieved great fortunes, and won success, by toiling hard at first, and then by trading and bargaining and getting ahead of other men.

"Well," said Luke, to himself, as he stood at the door, "I could do that too. Without doubt I also am one of the men who can do things. They did not work any harder than I do. But they got better pay. I am twenty-five. For ten years I have worked hard, and what have I got for it? This!"

He stepped out into the morning, alert and vigorous, deep-chested and straight-hipped. The strength of the hills had gone into him, and his eyes were bright with health. His kingdom was spread before him. There along the River of Meadows were the haunts of the moose and the caribou where he hunted in the fall; and yonder on the burnt hills around the great lake were the places where he watched for the bears; and up beside the River of Rocks ran his line of traps, swinging back by secret ways to many a nameless pond and hidden beaver-meadow; and all along the streams, when the ice went out in the spring, the great trout would be leaping in rapid and pool. Among the peaks and valleys of that forest-clad kingdom he could find his way as easily as a merchant walks from his house to his office. The secrets of bird and beast were known to him; every season of the year brought him its own tribute; the woods were his domain, vast, inexhaustible, free.

Here was his home, his cabin that he had built with his own hands. The roof was tight, the walls were well chinked with moss. It was snug and warm. But small—how pitifully small it looked to-day—and how lonely!

His hand-sledge stood beside the door, and against it leaned the axe. He caught it up and began to split wood for the stove. "No!" he cried, throwing down the axe, "I'm tired of this. It has lasted long enough. I'm going out to make my way in the world."

A couple of hours later, the sledge was packed

with camp-gear and bundles of skins. The door of
the cabin was shut; a ghostlike wreath of blue
smoke curled from the chimney. Luke stood, in his
snowshoes, on the white surface of the River of the
Way Out. He turned to look back for a moment,
and waved his hand.

"Good-bye, old cabin! Good-bye, the rivers!
Good-bye, the woods!"

II

The House on the Main Street

ALL the good houses in Scroll-Saw City were different, in the number and shape of the curious pinnacles that rose from their roofs and in the trim-
mings of their verandas. Yet they were all alike,
too, in their general expression of putting their
best foot foremost and feeling quite sure that they
made a brave show. They had lace curtains in their
front parlour windows, and outside of the curtains
were large red and yellow pots of artificial flowers
and indestructible palms and vulcanised rubber-
plants. It was a gay sight.

137

But by far the bravest of these houses was the residence of Mr. Matthew Wilson, the principal merchant of Scroll-Saw City. It stood on a corner of Main Street, glancing slyly out of the tail of one eye, side-ways down the street, toward the shop and the business, but keeping a bold, complacent front toward the street-cars and the smaller houses across the way. It might well be satisfied with itself, for it had three more pinnacles than any of its neighbours, and the work of the scroll-saw was looped and festooned all around the eaves and por- ticoes and bay-windows in amazing richness. More- over, in the front yard were cast-iron images painted white: a stag reposing on a door-mat; Diana properly dressed and returning from the chase; a small iron boy holding over his head a parasol from the ferrule of which a fountain squirted. The paths were of asphalt, gray and gritty in winter, but now, in the summer heat, black and pulpy to the tread.

There were many feet passing over them this afternoon, for Mr. and Mrs. Matthew Wilson were giving a reception to celebrate the official entrance

"Good-bye, old cabin! Good-bye, the rivers! Good-bye, the woods!"

of their daughter Amanda into a social life which she had permeated unofficially for several years. The house was sizzling full of people. Those who were jammed in the parlour tried to get into the dining-room, and those who were packed in the dining-room struggled to escape, holding plates of stratified cake and liquefied ice-cream high above their neighbours' heads like signals of danger and distress. Everybody was talking at the same time, in a loud, shrill voice, and nobody listened to what anybody else was saying. But it did not matter, for they all said the same things.

"Elegant house for a party, so full of—" "How perfectly lovely Amanda Wilson looks in that—" "Awfully warm day! Were you at the Tompkins' last—" "Wilson's Emporium must be doing good business to keep up all this—" "Hear he's going to enlarge the store and take Luke Woods into the—" "Shouldn't wonder if there might be a wedding here before next—"

The tide of chatter rose and swelled and ebbed and suddenly sank away. At six o'clock, the minister and two maiden ladies in black silk with lilac ribbons, laid down their last plates of ice-cream and said they thought they must be going. Amanda and her mother preened their dresses and patted their hair. " Come into the study," said Mr. Wilson to Luke. "I want to have a talk with you."

The little bookless room, called the study, was the one that kept its eye on the shop and the business, away down the street. You could see the brick front, and the plate-glass windows, and part of the gilt sign.

"Pretty good store," said Mr. Wilson, jingling the keys in his pocket, "does the biggest trade in the county, biggest but one in the whole state, I guess. And I must say, Luke Woods, you've done your share, these last five years, in building it up. Never had a clerk work so hard and so steady. You've got good business sense, I guess."

"I'm glad you think so," said Luke. "I did as well as I could."

"Yes," said the elder man, "and now I'm about ready to take you in with me, give you a share in the business. I want some one to help me run it, make it larger. We can double it, easy, if we stick to it and spread out. No reason why you shouldn't make a fortune out of it, and have a house just like this on the other corner, when you're my age."

Luke's thoughts were wandering a little. They went out from the stuffy room, beyond the dusty street, and the jangling cars, and the gilt sign, and the shop full of dry-goods and notions, and the high desks in the office—out to the dim, cool forest, where Snowberry and Partridge-berry and Wood-Magic grow. He heard the free winds rushing over the tree-tops, and saw the trail winding away before him in the green shade.

"You are very kind," said he, "I hope you will not be disappointed in me. Sometimes I think, per-haps—"

"Not at all, not at all," said the other. "It's all right. You're well fitted for it. And then, there's another thing. I guess you like my daughter Amanda pretty well. Eh? I've watched you, young man. I've had my eye on you! Now, of course, I can't say much about it—never can be sure of these kind of things, you know—but if you and she—"

The voice went on rolling out words complacently. But something strange was working in Luke's blood, and other voices were sounding faintly in his ears. He heard the lisping of the leaves on the little poplar-trees, the whistle of the black duck's wings as he circled in the air, the distant drumming of the grouse on his log, the rumble of the water-fall in the River of Rocks. The spray cooled his face. He saw the fish rising along the pool, and a stag feeding among the lily-pads.

"I don't know how to thank you, Mr. Wilson," said he at last, when the elder man stopped talking. "You have certainly treated me most generously. The only question is, whether— But to-morrow night, I think, with your consent, I will speak to your daughter. To-night I am going down to the store; there is a good deal of work to do on the books."

But when Luke came to the store, he did not go in. He walked along the street till he came to the river.

The water-side was strangely deserted. Everybody was at supper. A couple of schooners were moored at the wharf. The Portland steamer had

gone out. The row-boats hung idle at their little dock. Down the river, drifting and dancing
lightly over the opalescent ripples, following the
gentle turns of the current which flowed past the
end of the dock where Luke was standing, came a
white canoe, empty and astray.

III

The White Canoe

"THAT looks just like my old canoe," said he.
"Somebody must have left it adrift up the river.
I wonder how it floated down here without being
picked up." He put out his hand and caught it, as
it touched the dock.

In the stern a good paddle of maple-wood was
lying; in the middle there was a roll of blankets
and a pack of camp-stuff; in the bow a rifle.

"All ready for a trip," he laughed. "Nobody
going but me? Well, then, *au large!*" And stepping into the canoe he pushed out on the river.

The saffron and golden lights in the sky diffused
themselves over the surface of the water, and

143

spread from the bow of the canoe in deeper waves of purple and orange, as he paddled swiftly up stream. The pale yellow gas-lamps of the town faded behind him. The lumber-yards and factories and disconsolate little houses of the outskirts seemed to melt away. In a little while he was floating between dark walls of forest, through the heart of the wilderness.

The night deepened around him and the sky hung out its thousand lamps. Odours of the woods floated on the air: the spicy fragrance of the firs; the breath of hidden banks of twin-flower. Musk-rats swam noiselessly in the shadows, diving with a great commotion as the canoe ran upon them suddenly. A horned owl hooted from the branch of a dead pine-tree; far back in the forest a fox barked twice. The moon crept up behind the wall of trees and touched the stream with silver.

Presently the forest receded: the banks of the river grew broad and open; the dew glistened on the tall grass; it was surely the River of Meadows. Far ahead of him in a bend of the stream, Luke's ear caught a new sound: *slosh, slosh, slosh,* as if some heavy animal were crossing the wet meadow. Then a great splash! Luke swung the canoe into the shadow of the bank and paddled fast. As he turned the point a black bear came out of the river, and stood on the shore, shaking the water around him in glittering spray. *Ping!* said the rifle, and the bear fell. "Good luck!" said Luke. "I haven't forgotten how, after all. I'll take him into the canoe, and dress him up at the camp."

Yes, there was the little cabin at the meeting of the rivers. The door was padlocked, but Luke knew how to pry off one of the staples. Squirrels had made a litter on the floor, but that was soon swept out, and a fire crackled in the stove. There was tea and ham and bread in the pack in the canoe. Supper never tasted better. "One more night in the old camp," said Luke as he rolled himself in the blanket and dropped asleep in a moment.

The sun shone in at the door and woke him. "I must have a trout for breakfast," he cried, "there's one waiting for me at the mouth of Alder Brook, I suppose." So he caught up his rod from behind the door, and got into the canoe and paddled up the

River of Rocks. There was the broad, dark pool, like a little lake, with a rapid running in at the head, and close beside the rapid, the mouth of the brook. He sent his fly out by the edge of the alders. There was a huge swirl on the water, and the great-grandfather of all the trout in the river was hooked. Up and down the pool he played for half an hour, until at last the fight was over, and for want of a net Luke beached him on the gravel bank at the foot of the pool.

"Seven pounds if it's an ounce," said he. "This is my lucky day. Now all I need is some good meat to provision the camp."

He glanced down the river, and on the second point below the pool he saw a great black bull-moose with horns five feet wide.

Quietly, swiftly, the canoe went gliding down the stream; and ever as it crept along, the moose loped easily before it, from point to point, from bay to bay, past the little cabin, down the River of the Way Out, now rustling unseen through a bank of tall alders, now standing out for a moment bold and black on a beach of white sand—so all day long the moose loped down the stream and the white canoe followed. Just as the setting sun was poised above the trees, the great bull stopped and stood with head lifted. Luke pushed the canoe as near as he dared, and looked down for the rifle. He had left it at the cabin! The moose tossed his huge antlers, grunted, and stepped quietly over the bushes into the forest.

Luke paddled on down the stream. It occurred to him, suddenly, that it was near evening. He wondered a little how he should reach home in time for his engagement. But it did not seem strange, as he went swiftly on with the river, to see the first houses of the town, and the lumber-yards, and the schooners at the wharf.

He made the canoe fast at the dock, and went up the Main Street. There was the old shop, but the sign over it read, "Wilson and Woods Company, The Big Store." He went on to the house with the white iron images in the front yard. Diana was still returning from the chase. The fountain still squirted from the point of the little boy's parasol.

On the veranda sat a stout man in a rocking

chair, reading the newspaper. At the side of the house two little girls with pig-tails were playing croquet. Some one in the parlour was executing "After the Ball is Over" on a mechanical piano.

Luke accosted a stranger who passed him. "Excuse me, but can you tell me whether this is Mr. Matthew Wilson's house?"

"It used to be," said the stranger, "but old man Wilson has been dead these ten years."

"And who lives here now?" asked Luke.

"Mr. Woods: he married Wilson's daughter," said the stranger, and went on his way.

"Well," said Luke to himself, "this is just a little queer. Woods was my name for a while, when I lived here, but now, I suppose, I'm Luke Dubois again. Dashed if I can understand it. Somebody must have been dreaming."

So he went back to the white canoe, and paddled away up the river, and nobody in Scroll-Saw City ever set eyes on him again.

THE OTHER WISE MAN

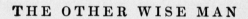

THE OTHER WISE MAN

YOU know the story of the Three Wise Men of the East, and how they travelled from far away to offer their gifts at the manger-cradle in Bethlehem. But have you ever heard the story of the Other Wise Man, who also saw the star in its rising, and set out to follow it, yet did not arrive with his brethren in the presence of the young child Jesus? Of the great desire of this fourth pilgrim, and how it was denied, yet accomplished in the denial; of his many wanderings and the probations of his soul; of the long way of his seeking and the strange way of his finding the One whom he sought—I would tell the tale as I have heard fragments of it in the Hall of Dreams, in the palace of the Heart of Man.

I

IN the days when Augustus Cæsar was master of many kings and Herod reigned in Jerusalem, there lived in the city of Ecbatana, among the mountains of Persia, a certain man named Artaban. His house stood close to the outermost of the walls which encircled the royal treasury. From his roof he could look over the seven-fold battlements of black and white and crimson and blue and red and silver and gold, to the hill where the summer palace of the Parthian emperors glittered like a jewel in a crown.

Around the dwelling of Artaban spread a fair garden, a tangle of flowers and fruit-trees, watered by a score of streams descending from the slopes of Mount Orontes, and made musical by innumerable birds. But all colour was lost in the soft and odorous darkness of the late September night, and all sounds were hushed in the deep charm of its silence, save the plashing of the water, like a voice half-sobbing and half-laughing under the shadows. High above the trees a dim glow of light shone through the curtained arches of the upper chamber, where the master of the house was holding council with his friends.

He stood by the doorway to greet his guests —a tall, dark man of about forty years, with brilliant eyes set near together under his broad brow, and firm lines graven around his fine, thin lips; the brow of a dreamer and the mouth of a soldier, a man of sensitive feeling but inflexible will—one of those who, in whatever age they may live, are born for inward conflict and a life of quest.

His robe was of pure white wool, thrown over a tunic of silk; and a white, pointed cap, with long lapels at the sides, rested on his flowing black hair. It was the dress of the ancient priesthood of the Magi, called the fire-worshippers.

"Welcome!" he said, in his low, pleasant voice, as one after another entered the room—"welcome, Abdus; peace be with you, Rhodaspes and Tigranes, and with you my father, Abgarus. You are all welcome. This house grows bright with the joy of your presence."

There were nine of the men, differing widely in age, but alike in the richness of their dress of many-coloured silks, and in the massive golden collars around their necks, marking them as Parthian nobles, and in the winged circles of gold resting upon their breasts, the sign of the followers of Zoroaster.

They took their places around a small black altar at the end of the room, where a tiny flame was burning. Artaban, standing beside it, and waving a barsom of thin tamarisk branches above the fire, fed it with dry sticks of pine and fragrant oils. Then he began the ancient chant of the Yasna, and the voices of his companions joined in the hymn to Ahura-Mazda:

> *We worship the Spirit Divine,*
> > *all wisdom and goodness possessing,*
> *Surrounded by Holy Immortals,*
> > *the givers of bounty and blessing;*
> *We joy in the work of His hands,*
> > *His truth and His power confessing.*
>
> *We praise all the things that are pure,*
> > *for these are His only Creation;*
> *The thoughts that are true, and the words*
> > *and the deeds that have won approbation;*
> *These are supported by Him,*
> > *and for these we make adoration.*

THE OTHER WISE MAN

Hear us, O Mazda ! Thou livest
      in truth and in heavenly gladness ;
Cleanse us from falsehood, and keep us
      from evil and bondage to badness ;
Pour out the light and the joy of Thy life
      on our darkness and sadness.

Shine on our gardens and fields,
      shine on our working and weaving ;
Shine on the whole race of man,
      believing and unbelieving ;
   Shine on us now through the night,
   Shine on us now in Thy might,
The flame of our holy love
      and the song of our worship receiving.

The fire rose with the chant, throbbing as if
the flame responded to the music, until it cast a
bright illumination through the whole apartment,
revealing its simplicity and splendour.

The floor was laid with tiles of dark blue veined
with white; pilasters of twisted silver stood out
against the blue walls; the clear-story of round-
arched windows above them was hung with azure
silk; the vaulted ceiling was a pavement of blue

stones, like the body of heaven in its clearness, sown with silver stars. From the four corners of the roof hung four golden magic-wheels, called the tongues of the gods. At the eastern end, behind the altar, there were two dark-red pillars of porphyry; above them a lintel of the same stone, on which was carved the figure of a winged archer, with his arrow set to the string and his bow drawn.

The doorway between the pillars, which opened upon the terrace of the roof, was covered with a heavy curtain of the colour of a ripe pomegranate, embroidered with innumerable golden rays shooting upward from the floor. In effect the room was like a quiet, starry night, all azure and silver, flushed in the east with rosy promise of the dawn. It was, as the house of a man should be, an expression of the character and spirit of the master.

He turned to his friends when the song was ended, and invited them to be seated on the divan at the western end of the room.

"You have come to-night," said he, looking around the circle, "at my call, as the faithful scholars of Zoroaster, to renew your worship and rekindle your faith in the God of Purity, even as this fire has been rekindled on the altar. We worship not the fire, but Him of whom it is the chosen symbol, because it is the purest of all created things. It speaks to us of one who is Light and Truth. Is it not so, my father?"

"It is well said, my son," answered the venerable Abgarus. "The enlightened are never idolaters. They lift the veil of form and go in to the shrine of reality, and new light and truth are coming to them continually through the old symbols."

"Hear me, then, my father and my friends," said Artaban, "while I tell you of the new light and truth that have come to me through the most ancient of all signs. We have searched the secrets of Nature together, and studied the healing virtues of water and fire and the plants. We have read also the books of prophecy in which the future is dimly foretold in words that are hard to understand. But the highest of all learning is the knowledge of the stars. To trace their course is to untangle the threads of the mystery of life from the beginning to the end. If we could follow them perfectly, nothing would be hidden from us. But is not our knowledge of them still incomplete? Are there not many stars still beyond our horizon —lights that are known only to the dwellers in the far south-land, among the spice-trees of Punt and the gold mines of Ophir?"

There was a murmur of assent among the listeners.

"The stars," said Tigranes, "are the thoughts of the Eternal. They are numberless. But the thoughts of man can be counted, like the years of his life. The wisdom of the Magi is the greatest of all wisdoms on earth, because it knows its own ignorance. And that is the secret of power. We keep men always looking and waiting for a new sunrise. But we ourselves understand that the darkness is equal to the light, and that the conflict between them will never be ended."

"That does not satisfy me," answered Arta-ban, "for, if the waiting must be endless, if there could be no fulfilment of it, then it would not be wisdom to look and wait. We should become like those new teachers of the Greeks, who say that there is no truth, and that the only wise men are those who spend their lives in discovering and exposing the lies that have been believed in the world. But the new sunrise will certainly appear in the appointed time. Do not our own books tell us that this will come to pass, and that men will see the brightness of a great light?"

"That is true," said the voice of Abgarus; "every faithful disciple of Zoroaster knows the prophecy of the Avesta, and carries the word in his heart. 'In that day Sosiosh the Victorious shall arise out of the number of the prophets in the east country. Around him shall shine a mighty brightness, and he shall make life everlasting, incorruptible, and immortal, and the dead shall rise again.' "

"This is a dark saying," said Tigranes, "and it may be that we shall never understand it. It is better to consider the things that are near at hand, and to increase the influence of the Magi in their own country, rather than to look for one who may be a stranger, and to whom we must resign our power."

The others seemed to approve these words. There was a silent feeling of agreement manifest among them; their looks responded with that indefinable expression which always follows when a speaker has uttered the thought that has been slumbering in the hearts of his listeners. But Artaban turned to Abgarus with a glow on his face, and said:

"My father, I have kept this prophecy in the secret place of my soul. Religion without a great hope would be like an altar without a living fire. And now the flame has burned more brightly, and by the light of it I have read other words which also have come from the fountain of Truth, and speak yet more clearly of the rising of the Victorious One in his brightness."

He drew from the breast of his tunic two small rolls of fine parchment, with writing upon them, and unfolded them carefully upon his knee.

"In the years that are lost in the past, long before our fathers came into the land of Babylon, there were wise men in Chaldea, from whom the first of the Magi learned the secret of the heavens.

And of these Balaam the son of Beor was one of the mightiest. Hear the words of his prophecy: 'There shall come a star out of Jacob, and a sceptre shall arise out of Israel.' "

The lips of Tigranes drew downward with contempt, as he said:

"Judah was a captive by the waters of Babylon, and the sons of Jacob were in bondage to our kings. The tribes of Israel are scattered through the mountains like lost sheep, and from the remnant that dwells in Judea under the yoke of Rome neither star nor sceptre shall arise."

"And yet," answered Artaban, "it was the Hebrew Daniel, the mighty searcher of dreams, the counsellor of kings, the wise Belteshazzar, who was most honoured and beloved of our great King Cyrus. A prophet of sure things and a reader of the thoughts of the Eternal, Daniel proved himself to our people. And these are the words that he wrote." (Artaban read from the second roll:) " 'Know, therefore, and understand that from the going forth of the commandment to restore Jerusalem, unto the Anointed One, the

Prince, the time shall be seven and threescore and two weeks.' "

"But, my son," said Abgarus, doubtfully, "these are mystical numbers. Who can interpret them, or who can find the key that shall unlock their meaning?"

Artaban answered: "It has been shown to me and to my three companions among the Magi— Caspar, Melchior, and Balthazar. We have searched the ancient tablets of Chaldea and computed the time. It falls in this year. We have studied the sky, and in the spring of the year we saw two of the greatest planets draw near together in the sign of the Fish, which is the house of the Hebrews. We also saw a new star there, which shone for one night and then vanished. Now again the two great planets are meeting. This night is their conjunction. My three brothers are watching by the ancient Temple of the Seven Spheres, at Borsippa, in Babylonia, and I am watching here. If the star shines again, they will wait ten days for me at the temple, and then we will set out together for Jerusalem, to see and wor-

THE OTHER WISE MAN

ship the promised one who shall be born King of Israel. I believe the sign will come. I have made ready for the journey. I have sold my possessions, and bought these three jewels—a sapphire, a ruby, and a pearl—to carry them as tribute to the King. And I ask you to go with me on the pilgrimage, that we may have joy together in finding the Prince who is worthy to be served."

While he was speaking he thrust his hand into the inmost fold of his girdle and drew out three great gems—one blue as a fragment of the night sky, one redder than a ray of sunrise, and one as pure as the peak of a snow-mountain at twilight—and laid them on the outspread scrolls before him.

But his friends looked on with strange and alien eyes. A veil of doubt and mistrust came over their faces, like a fog creeping up from the marshes to hide the hills. They glanced at each other with looks of wonder and pity, as those who have listened to incredible sayings, the story of a wild vision, or the proposal of an impossible enterprise.

At last Tigranes said: "Artaban, this is a vain dream. It comes from too much looking upon the stars and the cherishing of lofty thoughts. It would be wiser to spend the time in gathering money for the new fire-temple at Chala. No king will ever rise from the broken race of Israel, and no end will ever come to the eternal strife of light and darkness. He who looks for it is a chaser of shadows. Farewell."

And another said: "Artaban, I have no knowledge of these things, and my office as guardian of the royal treasure binds me here. The quest is not for me. But if thou must follow it, fare thee well."

And another said: "In my house there sleeps a new bride, and I cannot leave her nor take her with me on this strange journey. This quest is not for me. But may thy steps be prospered wherever thou goest. So, farewell."

And another said: "I am ill and unfit for hardship, but there is a man among my servants whom I will send with thee when thou goest, to bring me word how thou farest."

So, one by one, they left the house of Artaban. But Abgarus, the oldest and the one who loved him the best, lingered after the others had gone, and said, gravely: "My son, it may be that the light of truth is in this sign that has appeared in the skies, and then it will surely lead to the Prince and the mighty brightness. Or it may be that it is only a shadow of the light, as Tigranes has said, and then he who follows it will have a long pilgrimage and a fruitless search. But it is better to follow even the shadow of the best than to remain content with the worst. And those who would see wonderful things must often be ready to travel alone. I am too old for this journey, but my heart shall be a companion of thy pilgrimage day and night, and I shall know the end of thy quest. Go in peace."

Then Abgarus went out of the azure chamber with its silver stars, and Artaban was left in solitude.

He gathered up the jewels and replaced them in his girdle. For a long time he stood and watched the flame that flickered and sank upon the altar.

Then he crossed the hall, lifted the heavy curtain, and passed out between the pillars of porphyry to the terrace on the roof.

The shiver that runs through the earth ere she rouses from her night-sleep had already begun, and the cool wind that heralds the daybreak was drawing downward from the lofty snow-traced ravines of Mount Orontes. Birds, half-awakened, crept and chirped among the rustling leaves, and the smell of ripened grapes came in brief wafts from the arbours.

Far over the eastern plain a white mist stretched like a lake. But where the distant peaks of Zagros serrated the western horizon the sky was clear. Jupiter and Saturn rolled together like drops of lambent flame about to blend in one.

As Artaban watched them, a steel-blue spark was born out of the darkness beneath, rounding itself with purple splendours to a crimson sphere, and spiring upward through rays of saffron and orange into a point of white radiance. Tiny and infinitely remote, yet perfect in every part, it pulsated in the enormous vault as if the three jewels in the Magian's girdle had mingled and been transformed into a living heart of light.

He bowed his head. He covered his brow with his hands.

"It is the sign," he said. "The King is coming, and I will go to meet him."

II

ALL night long, Vasda, the swiftest of Artaban's horses, had been waiting, saddled and bridled, in her stall, pawing the ground impatiently, and shaking her bit as if she shared the eagerness of her master's purpose, though she knew not its meaning.

Before the birds had fully roused to their strong, high, joyful chant of morning song, before the white mist had begun to lift lazily from the plain, the Other Wise Man was in the saddle, riding swiftly along the high-road, which skirted the base of Mount Orontes, westward.

167

How close, how intimate is the comradeship between a man and his favourite horse on a long journey. It is a silent, comprehensive friendship, an intercourse beyond the need of words.

They drink at the same way-side springs, and sleep under the same guardian stars. They are conscious together of the subduing spell of nightfall and the quickening joy of daybreak. The master shares his evening meal with his hungry companion, and feels the soft, moist lips caressing the palm of his hand as they close over the morsel of bread. In the gray dawn he is roused from his bivouac by the gentle stir of a warm, sweet breath over his sleeping face, and looks up into the eyes of his faithful fellow-traveller, ready and waiting for the toil of the day. Surely, unless he is a pagan and an unbeliever, by whatever name he calls upon his God, he will thank Him for this voiceless sympathy, this dumb affection, and his morning prayer will embrace a double blessing—God bless us both, the horse and the rider, and keep our feet from falling and our souls from death!

Then, through the keen morning air, the swift hoofs beat their tattoo along the road, keeping time to the pulsing of two hearts that are moved with the same eager desire—to conquer space, to devour the distance, to attain the goal of the journey.

Artaban must indeed ride wisely and well if he would keep the appointed hour with the other Magi; for the route was a hundred and fifty parasangs, and fifteen was the utmost that he could travel in a day. But he knew Vasda's strength, and pushed forward without anxiety, making the fixed distance every day, though he must travel late into the night, and in the morning long before sunrise.

He passed along the brown slopes of Mount Orontes, furrowed by the rocky courses of a hundred torrents.

He crossed the level plains of the Nisæans, where the famous herds of horses, feeding in the wide pastures, tossed their heads at Vasda's approach, and galloped away with a thunder of many hoofs, and flocks of wild birds rose suddenly

169

from the swampy meadows, wheeling in great circles with a shining flutter of innumerable wings and shrill cries of surprise.

He traversed the fertile fields of Concabar, where the dust from the threshing-floors filled the air with a golden mist, half hiding the huge temple of Astarte with its four hundred pillars.

At Baghistan, among the rich gardens watered by fountains from the rock, he looked up at the mountain thrusting its immense rugged brow out over the road, and saw the figure of King Darius trampling upon his fallen foes, and the proud list of his wars and conquests graven high upon the face of the eternal cliff.

Over many a cold and desolate pass, crawling painfully across the wind-swept shoulders of the hills; down many a black mountain-gorge, where the river roared and raced before him like a savage guide; across many a smiling vale, with terraces of yellow limestone full of vines and fruit-trees; through the oak-groves of Carine and the dark Gates of Zagros, walled in by precipices; into the ancient city of Chala, where the people of

Samaria had been kept in captivity long ago; and
out again by the mighty portal, riven through
the encircling hills, where he saw the image of the
High Priest of the Magi sculptured on the wall
of rock, with hand uplifted as if to bless the centuries of pilgrims; past the entrance of the narrow defile, filled from end to end with orchards
of peaches and figs, through which the river
Gyndes foamed down to meet him; over the broad
rice-fields, where the autumnal vapours spread
their deathly mists; following along the course of
the river, under tremulous shadows of poplar and
tamarind, among the lower hills; and out upon
the flat plain, where the road ran straight as an
arrow through the stubble-fields and parched
meadows; past the city of Ctesiphon, where the
Parthian emperors reigned, and the vast metrop-
olis of Seleucia which Alexander built; across
the swirling floods of Tigris and the many channels of Euphrates, flowing yellow through the
corn-lands—Artaban pressed onward until he arrived, at nightfall on the tenth day, beneath the
shattered walls of populous Babylon.

Vasda was almost spent, and Artaban would gladly have turned into the city to find rest and refreshment for himself and for her. But he knew that it was three hours' journey yet to the Temple of the Seven Spheres, and he must reach the place by midnight if he would find his comrades waiting. So he did not halt, but rode steadily across the stubble-fields.

A grove of date-palms made an island of gloom in the pale yellow sea. As she passed into the shadow Vasda slackened her pace, and began to pick her way more carefully.

Near the farther end of the darkness an access of caution seemed to fall upon her. She scented some danger or difficulty; it was not in her heart to fly from it—only to be prepared for it, and to meet it wisely, as a good horse should do. The grove was close and silent as the tomb; not a leaf rustled, not a bird sang.

She felt her steps before her delicately, carrying her head low, and sighing now and then with apprehension. At last she gave a quick breath of anxiety and dismay, and stood stock-still, quivering in every muscle, before a dark object in the shadow of the last palm-tree.

Artaban dismounted. The dim starlight revealed the form of a man lying across the road. His humble dress and the outline of his haggard face showed that he was probably one of the Hebrews who still dwelt in great numbers around the city. His pallid skin, dry and yellow as parchment, bore the mark of the deadly fever which ravaged the marsh-lands in autumn. The chill of death was in his lean hand, and, as Artaban released it, the arm fell back inertly upon the motionless breast.

He turned away with a thought of pity, leaving the body to that strange burial which the Magians deemed most fitting—the funeral of the desert, from which the kites and vultures rise on dark wings, and the beasts of prey slink furtively away. When they are gone there is only a heap of white bones on the sand.

But, as he turned, a long, faint, ghostly sigh came from the man's lips. The bony fingers gripped the hem of the Magian's robe and held him fast.

Artaban's heart leaped to his throat, not with fear, but with a dumb resentment at the importunity of this blind delay.

How could he stay here in the darkness to minister to a dying stranger? What claim had this unknown fragment of human life upon his compassion or his service? If he lingered but for an hour he could hardly reach Borsippa at the appointed time. His companions would think he had given up the journey. They would go without him. He would lose his quest.

But if he went on now, the man would surely die. If Artaban stayed, life might be restored. His spirit throbbed and fluttered with the urgency of the crisis. Should he risk the great reward of his faith for the sake of a single deed of charity? Should he turn aside, if only for a moment, from the following of the star, to give a cup of cold water to a poor, perishing Hebrew?

"God of truth and purity," he prayed, "direct me in the holy path, the way of wisdom which Thou only knowest."

Then he turned back to the sick man. Loosening

the grasp of his hand, he carried him to a little mound at the foot of the palm-tree.

He unbound the thick folds of the turban and opened the garment above the sunken breast. He brought water from one of the small canals near by, and moistened the sufferer's brow and mouth. He mingled a draught of one of those simple but potent remedies which he carried always in his girdle—for the Magians were physicians as well as astrologers—and poured it slowly between the colourless lips. Hour after hour he laboured as only a skilful healer of disease can do. At last the man's strength returned; he sat up and looked about him.

"Who art thou?" he said, in the rude dialect of the country, "and why hast thou sought me here to bring back my life?"

"I am Artaban the Magian, of the city of Ecbatana, and I am going to Jerusalem in search of one who is to be born King of the Jews, a great Prince and Deliverer of all men. I dare not delay any longer upon my journey, for the caravan that has waited for me may depart without me. But see, here is all that I have left of bread and wine, and here is a potion of healing herbs. When thy strength is restored thou canst find the dwellings of the Hebrews among the houses of Babylon."

The Jew raised his trembling hand solemnly to heaven.

"Now may the God of Abraham and Isaac and Jacob bless and prosper the journey of the merciful, and bring him in peace to his desired haven. Stay! I have nothing to give thee in return—only this: that I can tell thee where the Messiah must be sought. For our prophets have said that he should be born not in Jerusalem, but in Bethlehem of Judah. May the Lord bring thee in safety to that place, because thou hast had pity upon the sick."

It was already long past midnight. Artaban rode in haste, and Vasda, restored by the brief rest, ran eagerly through the silent plain and swam the channels of the river. She put forth the remnant of her strength, and fled over the ground like a gazelle.

But the first beam of the rising sun sent a long

176

shadow before her as she entered upon the final stadium of the journey, and the eyes of Artaban, anxiously scanning the great mound of Nimrod and the Temple of the Seven Spheres, could discern no trace of his friends.

The many-coloured terraces of black and orange and red and yellow and green and blue and white, shattered by the convulsions of nature, and crumbling under the repeated blows of human violence, still glittered like a ruined rainbow in the morning light.

Artaban rode swiftly around the hill. He dismounted and climbed to the highest terrace, looking out toward the west.

The huge desolation of the marshes stretched away to the horizon and the border of the desert. Bitterns stood by the stagnant pools and jackals skulked through the low bushes; but there was no sign of the caravan of the Wise Men, far or near.

At the edge of the terrace he saw a little cairn of broken bricks, and under them a piece of papyrus. He caught it up and read: "We have waited past

177

the midnight, and can delay no longer. We go to find the King. Follow us across the desert."

Artaban sat down upon the ground and covered his head in despair.

"How can I cross the desert," said he, "with no food and with a spent horse? I must return to Babylon, sell my sapphire, and buy a train of camels, and provision for the journey. I may never overtake my friends. Only God the merciful knows whether I shall not lose the sight of the King because I tarried to show mercy."

III

THERE was a silence in the Hall of Dreams, where I was listening to the story of the Other Wise Man. Through this silence I saw, but very dimly, his figure passing over the dreary undulations of the desert, high upon the back of his camel, rocking steadily onward like a ship over the waves.

The land of death spread its cruel net around him. The stony waste bore no fruit but briers and thorns. The dark ledges of rock thrust them-

178

selves above the surface here and there, like the bones of perished monsters. Arid and inhospitable mountain-ranges rose before him, furrowed with dry channels of ancient torrents, white and ghastly as scars on the face of nature. Shifting hills of treacherous sand were heaped like tombs along the horizon. By day, the fierce heat pressed its intolerable burden on the quivering air. No living creature moved on the dumb, swooning earth, but tiny jerboas scuttling through the parched bushes, or lizards vanishing in the clefts of the rock. By night the jackals prowled and barked in the distance, and the lion made the black ravines echo with his hollow roaring, while a bitter, blighting chill followed the fever of the day. Through heat and cold, the Magian moved steadily onward.

Then I saw the gardens and orchards of Damascus, watered by the streams of Abana and Pharpar, with their sloping swards inlaid with bloom, and their thickets of myrrh and roses. I saw the long, snowy ridge of Hermon, and the dark groves of cedars, and the valley of the Jordan, and the blue waters of the Lake of Galilee, and the fertile plain of Esdraelon, and the hills of Ephraim, and the highlands of Judah. Through all these I followed the figure of Artaban moving steadily onward, until he arrived at Bethlehem. And it was the third day after the three Wise Men had come to that place and had found Mary and Joseph, with the young child, Jesus, and had laid their gifts of gold and frankincense and myrrh at his feet.

Then the Other Wise Man drew near, weary, but full of hope, bearing his ruby and his pearl to offer to the King. "For now at last," he said, "I shall surely find him, though I be alone, and later than my brethren. This is the place of which the Hebrew exile told me that the prophets had spoken, and here I shall behold the rising of the great light. But I must inquire about the visit of my brethren, and to what house the star directed them, and to whom they presented their tribute."

The streets of the village seemed to be deserted, and Artaban wondered whether the men had all gone up to the hill-pastures to bring down their sheep. From the open door of a cottage he heard the sound of a woman's voice singing softly. He entered and found a young mother hushing her baby to rest. She told him of the strangers from the far East who had appeared in the village three days ago, and how they said that a star had guided them to the place where Joseph of Nazareth was lodging with his wife and her new-born child, and how they had paid reverence to the child and given him many rich gifts.

"But the travellers disappeared again," she continued, "as suddenly as they had come. We were afraid at the strangeness of their visit. We could not understand it. The man of Nazareth took the child and his mother, and fled away that same night secretly, and it was whispered that they were going to Egypt. Ever since, there has been a spell upon the village; something evil hangs over it. They say that the Roman soldiers are coming from Jerusalem to force a new tax from us, and the men have driven the flocks and herds far back among the hills, and hidden themselves to escape it."

Artaban listened to her gentle, timid speech, and the child in her arms looked up in his face and smiled, stretching out its rosy hands to grasp at the winged circle of gold on his breast. His heart warmed to the touch. It seemed like a greeting of love and trust to one who had journeyed long in loneliness and perplexity, fighting with his own doubts and fears, and following a light that was veiled in clouds.

"Why might not this child have been the promised Prince?" he asked within himself, as he touched its soft cheek. "Kings have been born ere now in lowlier houses than this, and the favourite of the stars may rise even from a cottage. But it has not seemed good to the God of wisdom to reward my search so soon and so easily. The one whom I seek has gone before me; and now I must follow the King to Egypt."

The young mother laid the baby in its cradle, and rose to minister to the wants of the strange guest that fate had brought into her house. She set food before him, the plain fare of peasants, but willingly offered, and therefore full of refresh-

ment for the soul as well as for the body. Artaban
accepted it gratefully; and, as he ate, the child
fell into a happy slumber, and murmured sweetly
in its dreams, and a great peace filled the room.

But suddenly there came the noise of a wild
confusion in the streets of the village, a shrieking
and wailing of women's voices, a clangour of
brazen trumpets and a clashing of swords, and
a desperate cry: "The soldiers! the soldiers of
Herod! They are killing our children."

The young mother's face grew white with terror. She clasped her child to her bosom, and
crouched motionless in the darkest corner of the
room, covering him with the folds of her robe,
lest he should wake and cry.

But Artaban went quickly and stood in the
doorway of the house. His broad shoulders filled
the portal from side to side, and the peak of his
white cap all but touched the lintel.

The soldiers came hurrying down the street
with bloody hands and dripping swords. At the
sight of the stranger in his imposing dress they
hesitated with surprise. The captain of the band

approached the threshold to thrust him aside. But Artaban did not stir. His face was as calm as though he were watching the stars, and in his eyes there burned that steady radiance before which even the half-tamed hunting leopard shrinks, and the bloodhound pauses in his leap. He held the soldier silently for an instant, and then said in a low voice:

"I am all alone in this place, and I am waiting to give this jewel to the prudent captain who will leave me in peace."

He showed the ruby, glistening in the hollow of his hand like a great drop of blood.

The captain was amazed at the splendour of the gem. The pupils of his eyes expanded with desire, and the hard lines of greed wrinkled around his lips. He stretched out his hand and took the ruby.

"March on!" he cried to his men, "there is no child here. The house is empty."

The clamour and the clang of arms passed down the street as the headlong fury of the chase sweeps by the secret covert where the trembling deer is hidden. Artaban re-entered the cottage. He turned his face to the east and prayed:

"God of truth, forgive my sin! I have said the thing that is not, to save the life of a child. And two of my gifts are gone. I have spent for man that which was meant for God. Shall I ever be worthy to see the face of the King?"

But the voice of the woman, weeping for joy in the shadow behind him, said very gently:

"Because thou hast saved the life of my little one, may the Lord bless thee and keep thee; the Lord make His face to shine upon thee and be gracious unto thee; the Lord lift up His countenance upon thee and give thee peace."

IV

AGAIN there was a silence in the Hall of Dreams, deeper and more mysterious than the first interval, and I understood that the years of Artaban were flowing very swiftly under the stillness, and I caught only a glimpse, here and there, of the river of his life shining through the mist that concealed its course.

THE BLUE FLOWER

I saw him moving among the throngs of men in populous Egypt, seeking everywhere for traces of the household that had come down from Bethlehem, and finding them under the spreading sycamore-trees of Heliopolis, and beneath the walls of the Roman fortress of New Babylon beside the Nile—traces so faint and dim that they vanished before him continually, as footprints on the wet river-sand glisten for a moment with moisture and then disappear.

I saw him again at the foot of the pyramids, which lifted their sharp points into the intense saffron glow of the sunset sky, changeless monuments of the perishable glory and the imperishable hope of man. He looked up into the face of the crouching Sphinx and vainly tried to read the meaning of the calm eyes and smiling mouth. Was it, indeed, the mockery of all effort and all aspiration, as Tigranes had said—the cruel jest of a riddle that has no answer, a search that never can succeed? Or was there a touch of pity and encouragement in that inscrutable smile—a promise that even the defeated should attain a victory, and the disappointed should discover a prize, and the ignorant should be made wise, and the blind should see, and the wandering should come into the haven at last?

I saw him again in an obscure house of Alexandria, taking counsel with a Hebrew rabbi. The venerable man, bending over the rolls of parchment on which the prophecies of Israel were written, read aloud the pathetic words which foretold the sufferings of the promised Messiah—the despised and rejected of men, the man of sorrows and acquainted with grief.

"And remember, my son," said he, fixing his eyes upon the face of Artaban, "the King whom thou seekest is not to be found in a palace, nor among the rich and powerful. If the light of the world and the glory of Israel had been appointed to come with the greatness of earthly splendour, it must have appeared long ago. For no son of Abraham will ever again rival the power which Joseph had in the palaces of Egypt, or the magnificence of Solomon throned between the lions in Jerusalem. But the light for which the world is waiting is a new light, the glory that shall rise out of patient and triumphant suffering. And the kingdom which is to be established forever is a new kingdom, the royalty of unconquerable love.

"I do not know how this shall come to pass, nor how the turbulent kings and peoples of earth shall be brought to acknowledge the Messiah and pay homage to him. But this I know. Those who seek him will do well to look among the poor and the lowly, the sorrowful and the oppressed."

So I saw the Other Wise Man again and again, travelling from place to place, and searching among the people of the dispersion, with whom the little family from Bethlehem might, perhaps, have found a refuge. He passed through countries where famine lay heavy upon the land, and the poor were crying for bread. He made his dwelling in plague-stricken cities where the sick were languishing in the bitter companionship of helpless misery. He visited the oppressed and the afflicted in the gloom of subterranean prisons, and the crowded wretchedness of slave-markets, and the weary toil of galley-ships. In all this populous and intricate world of anguish, though he found none to worship, he found many to help. He fed the hungry, and clothed the naked, and healed the sick, and comforted the captive; and his years passed more swiftly than the weaver's shuttle that flashes back and forth through the loom while the web grows and the pattern is completed.

It seemed almost as if he had forgotten his quest. But once I saw him for a moment as he stood alone at sunrise, waiting at the gate of a Roman prison. He had taken from a secret resting-place in his bosom the pearl, the last of his jewels. As he looked at it, a mellower lustre, a soft and iridescent light, full of shifting gleams of azure and rose, trembled upon its surface. It seemed to have absorbed some reflection of the lost sapphire and ruby. So the secret purpose of a noble life draws into itself the memories of past joy and past sorrow. All that has helped it, all that has hindered it, is transfused by a subtle magic into its very essence. It becomes more luminous and precious the longer it is carried close to the warmth of the beating heart.

189

Then, at last, while I was thinking of this pearl, and of its meaning, I heard the end of the story of the Other Wise Man.

V

THREE-AND-THIRTY years of the life of Artaban had passed away, and he was still a pilgrim and a seeker after light. His hair, once darker than the cliffs of Zagros, was now white as the wintry snow that covered them. His eyes, that once flashed like flames of fire, were dull as embers smouldering among the ashes.

Worn and weary and ready to die, but still looking for the King, he had come for the last time to Jerusalem. He had often visited the holy city before, and had searched all its lanes and crowded hovels and black prisons without finding any trace of the family of Nazarenes who had fled from Bethlehem long ago. But now it seemed as if he must make one more effort, and something whispered in his heart that, at last, he might succeed.

It was the season of the Passover. The city was thronged with strangers. The children of Israel,

190

scattered in far lands, had returned to the Temple for the great feast, and there had been a confusion of tongues in the narrow streets for many days.

But on this day a singular agitation was visible in the multitude. The sky was veiled with a portentous gloom. Currents of excitement seemed to flash through the crowd. A secret tide was sweeping them all one way. The clatter of sandals and the soft, thick sound of thousands of bare feet shuffling over the stones, flowed unceasingly along the street that leads to the Damascus gate.

Artaban joined a group of people from his own country, Parthian Jews who had come up to keep the Passover, and inquired of them the cause of the tumult, and where they were going.

"We are going," they answered, "to the place called Golgotha, outside the city walls, where there is to be an execution. Have you not heard what has happened? Two famous robbers are to be crucified, and with them another, called Jesus of Nazareth, a man who has done many wonderful works among the people, so that they love him greatly. But the priests and elders have said that he must die, because he gave himself out to be the Son of God. And Pilate has sent him to the cross because he said that he was the 'King of the Jews.'"

How strangely these familiar words fell upon the tired heart of Artaban! They had led him for a lifetime over land and sea. And now they came to him mysteriously, like a message of despair. The King had arisen, but he had been denied and cast out. He was about to perish. Perhaps he was already dying. Could it be the same who had been born in Bethlehem thirty-three years ago, at whose birth the star had appeared in heaven, and of whose coming the prophets had spoken?

Artaban's heart beat unsteadily with that troubled, doubtful apprehension which is the excitement of old age. But he said within himself: "The ways of God are stranger than the thoughts of men, and it may be that I shall find the King, at last, in the hands of his enemies, and shall come in time to offer my pearl for his ransom before he dies."

So the old man followed the multitude with slow and painful steps toward the Damascus gate of the city. Just beyond the entrance of the guardhouse a troop of Macedonian soldiers came down the street, dragging a young girl with torn dress and dishevelled hair. As the Magian paused to look at her with compassion, she broke suddenly from the hands of her tormentors, and threw herself at his feet, clasping him around the knees. She had seen his white cap and the winged circle on his breast.

"Have pity on me," she cried, "and save me, for the sake of the God of Purity! I also am a daughter of the true religion which is taught by the Magi. My father was a merchant of Parthia, but he is dead, and I am seized for his debts to be sold as a slave. Save me from worse than death!"

Artaban trembled.

It was the old conflict in his soul, which had come to him in the palm-grove of Babylon and in the cottage at Bethlehem—the conflict between the expectation of faith and the impulse of love. Twice the gift which he had consecrated to the

193

worship of religion had been drawn to the service of humanity. This was the third trial, the ultimate probation, the final and irrevocable choice.

Was it his great opportunity, or his last temptation? He could not tell. One thing only was clear in the darkness of his mind—it was inevitable. And does not the inevitable come from God?

One thing only was sure to his divided heart— to rescue this helpless girl would be a true deed of love. And is not love the light of the soul?

He took the pearl from his bosom. Never had it seemed so luminous, so radiant, so full of tender, living lustre. He laid it in the hand of the slave.

"This is thy ransom, daughter! It is the last of my treasures which I kept for the King."

While he spoke, the darkness of the sky deepened, and shuddering tremors ran through the earth heaving convulsively like the breast of one who struggles with mighty grief.

The walls of the houses rocked to and fro. Stones were loosened and crashed into the street.

Dust clouds filled the air. The soldiers fled in terror, reeling like drunken men. But Artaban and the girl whom he had ransomed crouched helpless beneath the wall of the Prætorium.

What had he to fear? What had he to hope? He had given away the last remnant of his tribute for the King. He had parted with the last hope of finding him. The quest was over, and it had failed. But, even in that thought, accepted and embraced, there was peace. It was not resignation. It was not submission. It was something more profound and searching. He knew that all was well, because he had done the best that he could from day to day. He had been true to the light that had been given to him. He had looked for more. And if he had not found it, if a failure was all that came out of his life, doubtless that was the best that was possible. He had not seen the revelation of "life everlasting, incorruptible and immortal." But he knew that even if he could live his earthly life over again, it could not be otherwise than it had been.

One more lingering pulsation of the earthquake

quivered through the ground. A heavy tile, shaken from the roof, fell and struck the old man on the temple. He lay breathless and pale, with his gray head resting on the young girl's shoulder, and the blood trickling from the wound. As she bent over him, fearing that he was dead, there came a voice through the twilight, very small and still, like music sounding from a distance, in which the notes are clear but the words are lost. The girl turned to see if some one had spoken from the window above them, but she saw no one.

Then the old man's lips began to move, as if in answer, and she heard him say in the Parthian tongue:

"Not so, my Lord! For when saw I thee an hungered and fed thee? Or thirsty, and gave thee drink? When saw I thee a stranger, and took thee in? Or naked, and clothed thee? When saw I thee sick or in prison, and came unto thee? Three-and-thirty years have I looked for thee; but I have never seen thy face, nor ministered to thee, my King."

He ceased, and the sweet voice came again. And

Then the old man's lips began to move.

again the maid heard it, very faint and far away. But now it seemed as though she understood the words:

"Verily I say unto thee, Inasmuch as thou hast done it unto one of the least of these my brethren, thou hast done it unto me."

A calm radiance of wonder and joy lighted the pale face of Artaban like the first ray of dawn on a snowy mountain-peak. A long breath of relief exhaled gently from his lips.

His journey was ended. His treasures were accepted. The Other Wise Man had found the King.

A HANDFUL OF CLAY

A HANDFUL OF CLAY

THERE was a handful of clay in the bank of a river. It was only common clay, coarse and heavy; but it had high thoughts of its own value, and wonderful dreams of the great place which it was to fill in the world when the time came for its virtues to be discovered.

Overhead, in the spring sunshine, the trees whispered together of the glory which descended upon them when the delicate blossoms and leaves began to expand, and the forest glowed with fair, clear colours, as if the dust of thousands of rubies and emeralds were hanging, in soft clouds, above the earth.

The flowers, surprised with the joy of beauty, bent their heads to one another, as the wind caressed them, and said: "Sisters, how lovely you have become. You make the day bright."

The river, glad of new strength and rejoicing in the unison of all its waters, murmured to the shores in music, telling of its release from icy fetters, its swift flight from the snow-clad mountains, and the mighty work to which it was hurrying— the wheels of many mills to be turned, and great ships to be floated to the sea.

Waiting blindly in its bed, the clay comforted itself with lofty hopes. "My time will come," it said. "I was not made to be hidden forever. Glory and beauty and honour are coming to me in due season."

One day the clay felt itself taken from the place where it had waited so long. A flat blade of iron passed beneath it, and lifted it, and tossed it into a cart with other lumps of clay, and it was carried far away, as it seemed, over a rough and stony road. But it was not afraid, nor discouraged, for it said to itself: "This is necessary. The path to glory is always rugged. Now I am on my way to play a great part in the world."

But the hard journey was nothing compared with the tribulation and distress that came after it. The clay was put into a trough and mixed and beaten and stirred and trampled. It seemed almost unbearable. But there was consolation in the

A HANDFUL OF CLAY

thought that something very fine and noble was certainly coming out of all this trouble. The clay felt sure that, if it could only wait long enough, a wonderful reward was in store for it.

Then it was put upon a swiftly turning wheel, and whirled around until it seemed as if it must fly into a thousand pieces. A strange power pressed it and moulded it, as it revolved, and through all the dizziness and pain it felt that it was taking a new form.

Then an unknown hand put it into an oven, and fires were kindled about it—fierce and penetrating —hotter than all the heats of summer that had ever brooded upon the bank of the river. But through all, the clay held itself together and endured its trials, in the confidence of a great future. "Surely," it thought, "I am intended for something very splendid, since such pains are taken with me. Perhaps I am fashioned for the ornament of a temple, or a precious vase for the table of a king."

At last the baking was finished. The clay was taken from the furnace and set down upon a board, in the cool air, under the blue sky. The tribulation was passed. The reward was at hand.

Close beside the board there was a pool of water, not very deep, nor very clear, but calm enough to reflect, with impartial truth, every image that fell upon it. There, for the first time, as it was lifted from the board, the clay saw its new shape, the reward of all its patience and pain, the consummation of its hopes—a common flower-pot, straight and stiff, red and ugly. And then it felt that it was not destined for a king's house, nor for a palace of art, because it was made without glory or beauty or honour; and it murmured against the unknown maker, saying, "Why hast thou made me thus?"

Many days it passed in sullen discontent. Then it was filled with earth, and something—it knew not what—but something rough and brown and dead-looking, was thrust into the middle of the earth and covered over. The clay rebelled at this new disgrace. "This is the worst of all that has happened to me, to be filled with dirt and rubbish. Surely I am a failure."

A HANDFUL OF CLAY

But presently it was set in a greenhouse, where the sunlight fell warm upon it, and water was sprinkled over it, and day by day as it waited, a change began to come to it. Something was stirring within it—a new hope. Still it was ignorant, and knew not what the new hope meant.

One day the clay was lifted again from its place, and carried into a great church. Its dream was coming true after all. It had a fine part to play in the world. Glorious music flowed over it. It was surrounded with flowers. Still it could not understand. So it whispered to another vessel of clay, like itself, close beside it, "Why have they set me here? Why do all the people look toward us?" And the other vessel answered, "Do you not know? You are carrying a royal sceptre of lilies. Their petals are white as snow, and the heart of them is like pure gold. The people look this way because the flower is the most wonderful in the world. And the root of it is in your heart."

Then the clay was content, and silently thanked its maker, because, though an earthen vessel, it held so great a treasure.

THE LOST WORD

THE LOST WORD

I

"COME down, Hermas, come down! The night is past. It is time to be stirring. Christ is born to-day. Peace be with you in His name. Make haste and come down!"

A little group of young men were standing in a street of Antioch, in the dusk of early morning, fifteen hundred years ago—a class of candidates who had nearly finished their years of training for the Christian church. They had come to call their fellow-student Hermas from his lodging.

Their voices rang out cheerily through the cool air. They were full of that glad sense of life which the young feel when they have risen early and come to rouse one who is still sleeping. There was a note of friendly triumph in their call, as if they were exulting unconsciously in having begun the adventure of the new day before their comrade.

But Hermas was not asleep. He had been waking for hours, and the walls of his narrow lodging had been a prison to his heart. A nameless sorrow and discontent had fallen upon him, and he could find no escape from the heaviness of his own thoughts.

There is a sadness of youth into which the old cannot enter. It seems unreal and causeless. But it is even more bitter and burdensome than the sadness of age. There is a sting of resentment in it, a fever of angry surprise that the world should so soon be a disappointment, and life so early take on the look of a failure. It has little reason in it, perhaps, but it has all the more weariness and gloom, because the man who is oppressed by it feels dimly that it is an unnatural thing that he should be tired of living before he has fairly begun to live.

Hermas had fallen into the very depths of this strange self-pity. He was out of tune with everything around him. He had been thinking, through the dead night, of all that he had given up when he left the house of his father, the wealthy pagan Demetrius, to join the company of the Christians. Only two years ago he had been one of the richest young men in Antioch. Now he was one of the poorest. The worst of it was that, though he had made the choice willingly and with a kind of enthusiasm, he was already dissatisfied with it.

The new life was no happier than the old. He was weary of vigils and fasts, weary of studies and penances, weary of prayers and sermons. He felt like a slave in a treadmill. He knew that he must go on. His honour, his conscience, his sense of duty, bound him. He could not go back to the old careless pagan life again; for something had happened within him which made a return impossible. Doubtless he had found the true religion, but he had found it only as a task and a burden; its joy and peace had slipped away from him.

He felt disillusioned and robbed. He sat beside his hard couch, waiting without expectancy for the gray dawn of another empty day, and hardly lifting his head at the shouts of his friends.

"Come down, Hermas, you sluggard! Come down! It is Christmas morn. Awake, and be glad with us!"

"I am coming," he answered listlessly; "only have patience a moment. I have been awake since midnight, and waiting for the day."

"You hear him!" said his friends one to another. "How he puts us all to shame! He is more watchful, more eager, than any of us. Our master, John the Presbyter, does well to be proud of him. He is the best man in our class."

While they were talking the door opened and Hermas stepped out. He was a figure to be remarked in any company—tall, broad-shouldered, straight-hipped, with a head proudly poised on the firm column of the neck, and short brown curls clustering over the square forehead. It was the perpetual type of vigorous and intelligent young manhood, such as may be found in every century among the throngs of ordinary men, as if to show what the flower of the race should be. But the light in his eyes was clouded and uncertain; his smooth cheeks were leaner than they should have been at twenty; and there were downward lines about his mouth which spoke of desires unsatisfied and ambitions repressed. He joined his companions with brief greetings,—a nod to one, a word to another,—and they passed together down the steep street.

Overhead the mystery of daybreak was silently transfiguring the sky. The curtain of darkness had lifted along the edge of the horizon. The ragged crests of Mount Silpius were outlined with pale saffron light. In the central vault of heaven a few large stars twinkled drowsily. The great city, still chiefly pagan, lay more than half-asleep. But multitudes of the Christians, dressed in white and carrying lighted torches in their hands, were hurrying toward the Basilica of Constantine to keep the new holy-day of the church, the festival of the birthday of their Master.

The vast, bare building was soon crowded, and the younger converts, who were not yet permitted to stand among the baptised, found it difficult to come to their appointed place between the first two pillars of the house, just within the threshold. There was some good-humoured pressing and jostling about the door; but the candidates pushed steadily forward.

"By your leave, friends, our station is beyond you. Will you let us pass? Many thanks."

A touch here, a courteous nod there, a little patience, a little persistence, and at last they stood in their place. Hermas was taller than his companions; he could look easily over their heads and survey the sea of people stretching away through the columns, under the shadows of the high roof, as the tide spreads on a calm day into the pillared cavern of Staffa, quiet as if the ocean hardly dared to breathe. The light of many flambeaux fell, in flickering, uncertain rays, over the assembly. At the end of the vista there was a circle of clearer, steadier radiance. Hermas could see the bishop in his great chair, surrounded by the presbyters, the lofty desks on either side for the readers of the Scripture, the communion-table and the table of offerings in the middle of the church.

The call to prayer sounded down the long aisle. Thousands of hands were joyously lifted in the air, as if the sea had blossomed into waving lilies, and the "Amen" was like the murmur of countless ripples in an echoing place.

Then the singing began, led by the choir of a hundred trained voices which the Bishop Paul had founded in Antioch. Timidly, at first, the music felt its way, as the people joined with a broken and uncertain cadence: the mingling of many little waves not yet gathered into rhythm and harmony. Soon the longer, stronger billows of song rolled in, sweeping from side to side as the men and the women answered in the clear antiphony.

Hermas had often been carried on those

Tides of music's golden sea
Setting toward eternity.

But to-day his heart was a rock that stood motionless. The flood passed by and left him unmoved.

Looking out from his place at the foot of the pillar, he saw a man standing far off in the lofty bema. Short and slender, wasted by sickness, gray before his time, with pale cheeks and wrinkled brow, he seemed at first like a person of no significance—a reed shaken in the wind. But there was a look in his deep-set, poignant eyes, as he gathered all the glances of the multitude to himself, that belied his mean appearance and prophesied power. Hermas knew very well who it was: the man who had drawn him from his father's house, the teacher who was instructing him as a son in the Christian faith, the guide and trainer of his soul—John of Antioch, whose fame filled the city and began to overflow Asia, and who was called already Chrysostom, the golden-mouthed preacher.

Hermas had felt the magic of his eloquence many a time; and to-day, as the tense voice vibrated through the stillness, and the sentences moved onward, growing fuller and stronger, bearing argosies of costly rhetoric and treasures of homely speech in their bosom, and drawing the hearts of men with a resistless magic, Hermas knew that the preacher had never been more potent, more inspired.

He played on that immense congregation as a master on an instrument. He rebuked their sins, and they trembled. He touched their sorrows, and they wept. He spoke of the conflicts, the triumphs, the glories of their faith, and they broke out in thunders of applause. He hushed them into reverent silence, and led them tenderly, with the wise men of the East, to the lowly birthplace of Jesus.

"Do thou, therefore, likewise leave the Jewish people, the troubled city, the bloodthirsty tyrant, the pomp of the world, and hasten to Bethlehem, the sweet house of spiritual bread. For though thou be but a shepherd, and come hither, thou shalt behold the young Child in an inn. Though thou be a king, and come not hither, thy purple robe shall profit thee nothing. Though thou be one of the wise men, this shall be no hindrance to thee. Only let thy coming be to honour and adore, with trembling joy, the Son of God, to whose name be glory, on this His birthday, and forever and forever."

The soul of Hermas did not answer to the musician's touch. The strings of his heart were slack and soundless; there was no response within him. He was neither shepherd, nor king, nor wise man; only an unhappy, dissatisfied, questioning youth. He was out of sympathy with the eager preacher, the joyous hearers. In their harmony he had no part. Was it for this that he had forsaken his inheritance and narrowed his life to poverty and hardship? What was it all worth?

The gracious prayers with which the young converts were blessed and dismissed before the sacrament sounded hollow in his ears. Never had he felt so utterly lonely as in that praying throng. He went out with his companions like a man departing from a banquet where all but he had been fed.

"Farewell, Hermas," they cried, as he turned from them at the door. But he did not look back, nor wave his hand. He was already alone in his heart.

When he entered the broad Avenue of the Colonnades, the sun had already topped the eastern hills, and the ruddy light was streaming through the long double row of archways and over the pavements of crimson marble. But Hermas turned his back to the morning, and walked with his shadow before him.

The street began to swarm and whirl and quiver with the motley life of a huge city: beggars and jugglers, dancers and musicians, gilded youths in their chariots, and daughters of joy looking out from their windows, all intoxicated with the mere delight of living and the gladness of a new day. The pagan populace of Antioch—reckless, pleasure-loving, spendthrift—were preparing for the Saturnalia. But all this Hermas had renounced. He cleft his way through the crowd slowly, like a reluctant swimmer weary of breasting the tide.

At the corner of the street where the narrow, populous Lane of the Camel-drivers crossed the Colonnades, a story-teller had bewitched a circle of people around him. It was the same old tale of love and adventure that many generations have listened to; but the lively fancy of the hearers lent it new interest, and the wit of the improviser drew forth sighs of interest and shouts of laughter.

A yellow-haired girl on the edge of the throng turned, as Hermas passed, and smiled in his face. She put out her hand and caught him by the sleeve.

"Stay," she said, "and laugh a bit with us. I know who you are—the son of Demetrius. You must have bags of gold. Why do you look so black? Love is alive yet."

Hermas shook off her hand, but not ungently.

"I don't know what you mean," he said. "You are mistaken in me. I am poorer than you are."

But as he passed on, he felt the warm touch of her fingers through the cloth on his arm. It seemed as if she had plucked him by the heart.

He went out by the Western Gate, under the golden cherubim that the Emperor Titus had stolen from the ruined Temple of Jerusalem and fixed upon the arch of triumph. He turned to the left, and climbed the hill to the road that led to the Grove of Daphne.

In all the world there was no other highway as beautiful. It wound for five miles along the foot of the mountains, among gardens and villas, plantations of myrtles and mulberries, with wide outlooks over the valley of Orontes and the distant, shimmering sea.

The richest of all the dwellings was the House

of the Golden Pillars, the mansion of Demetrius. He had won the favor of the apostate Emperor Julian, whose vain efforts to restore the worship of the heathen gods, some twenty years ago, had opened an easy way to wealth and power for all who would mock and oppose Christianity. Demetrius was not a sincere fanatic like his royal master; but he was bitter enough in his professed scorn of the new religion, to make him a favourite at the court where the old religion was in fashion. He had reaped a rich reward of his policy, and a strange sense of consistency made him more fiercely loyal to it than if it had been a real faith. He was proud of being called "the friend of Julian"; and when his son joined himself to the Christians, and acknowledged the unseen God, it seemed like an insult to his father's success. He drove the boy from his door and disinherited him.

The glittering portico of the serene, haughty house, the repose of the well-ordered garden, still blooming with belated flowers, seemed at once to deride and to invite the young outcast plodding along the dusty road. "This is your birthright," whispered the clambering rose-trees by the gate; and the closed portals of carven bronze said: "You have sold it for a thought—a dream."

II

HERMAS found the Grove of Daphne quite deserted. There was no sound in the enchanted vale but the rustling of the light winds chasing each other through the laurel thickets, and the babble of innumerable streams. Memories of the days and nights of delicate pleasure that the grove had often seen still haunted the bewildered paths and broken fountains. At the foot of a rocky eminence, crowned with the ruins of Apollo's temple, which had been mysteriously destroyed by fire just after Julian had restored and reconsecrated it, Hermas sat down beside a gushing spring, and gave himself up to sadness.

"How beautiful the world would be, how joyful, how easy to live in, without religion! These questions about unseen things, perhaps about unreal things, these restraints and duties and sacrifices—if I were only free from them all, and could only forget them all, then I could live my life as I pleased, and be happy."

"Why not?" said a quiet voice at his back.

He turned, and saw an old man with a long beard and a threadbare cloak (the garb affected by the pagan philosophers) standing behind him and smiling curiously.

"How is it that you answer that which has not been spoken?" said Hermas; "and who are you that honour me with your company?"

"Forgive the intrusion," answered the stranger; "it is not ill meant. A friendly interest is as good as an introduction."

"But to what singular circumstance do I owe this interest?"

"To your face," said the old man, with a courteous inclination. "Perhaps also a little to the fact that I am the oldest inhabitant here, and feel as if all visitors were my guests, in a way."

"Are you, then, one of the keepers of the grove? And have you given up your work with the trees to take a holiday as a philosopher?"

"Not at all. The robe of philosophy is a mere affectation, I must confess. I think little of it. My profession is the care of altars. In fact, I am the solitary priest of Apollo whom the Emperor Julian found here when he came to revive the worship of the grove, some twenty years ago. You have heard of the incident?"

"Yes," said Hermas, beginning to be interested; "the whole city must have heard of it, for it is still talked of. But surely it was a strange sacrifice that you brought to celebrate the restoration of Apollo's temple?"

"You mean the ancient goose?" said the old man laughing. "Well, perhaps it was not precisely what the emperor expected. But it was all that I had, and it seemed to me not inappropriate. You will agree to that if you are a Christian, as I guess from your dress."

"You speak lightly for a priest of Apollo."

"Oh, as for that, I am no bigot. The priesthood is a professional matter, and the name of Apollo is as good as any other. How many altars do you think there have been in this grove?"

"I do not know."

"Just four-and-twenty, including that of the martyr Babylas, whose ruined chapel you see just beyond us. I have had something to do with most of them in my time. They are transitory. They give employment to care-takers for a while. But the thing that lasts, and the thing that interests me, is the human life that plays around them. The game has been going on for centuries. It still disports itself very pleasantly on summer evenings through these shady walks. Believe me, for I know. Daphne and Apollo are shadows. But the flying maidens and the pursuing lovers, the music and the dances, these are realities. Life is a game, and the world keeps it up merrily. But you? You are of a sad countenance for one so young and so fair. Are you a loser in the game?"

The words and tone of the speaker fitted Hermas' mood as a key fits the lock. He opened his heart to the old man, and told him the story of his life: his luxurious boyhood in his father's house; the irresistible spell which compelled him to forsake it when he heard John's preaching of the new religion; his lonely year with the anchorites among the mountains; the strict discipline in his teacher's house at Antioch; his weariness of duty, his distaste for poverty, his discontent with worship.

"And to-day," said he, "I have been thinking that I am a fool. My life is swept as bare as a hermit's cell. There is nothing in it but a dream, a thought of God, which does not satisfy me."

The singular smile deepened on his companion's face. "You are ready, then," he suggested, "to renounce your new religion and go back to that of your father?"

"No; I renounce nothing, I accept nothing. I do not wish to think about it. I only wish to live."

"A very reasonable wish, and I think you are about to see its accomplishment. Indeed, I may even say that I can put you in the way of securing it. Do you believe in magic?"

"I do not know whether I believe in anything. This is not a day on which I care to make professions of faith. I believe in what I see. I want what will give me pleasure."

"Well," said the old man, soothingly, as he

plucked a leaf from the laurel-tree above them and dipped it in the spring, "let us dismiss the riddles of belief. I like them as little as you do. You know this is a Castalian fountain. The Emperor Hadrian once read his fortune here from a leaf dipped in the water. Let us see what this leaf tells us. It is already turning yellow. How do you read that?"

"Wealth," said Hermas, laughing, as he looked at his mean garments.

"And here is a bud on the stem that seems to be swelling. What is that?"

"Pleasure," answered Hermas, bitterly.

"And here is a tracing of wreaths upon the surface. What do you make of that?"

"What you will," said Hermas, not even taking the trouble to look. "Suppose we say success and fame?"

"Yes," said the stranger; "it is all written here. I promise that you shall enjoy it all. But you do not need to believe in my promise. I am not in the habit of requiring faith of those whom I would serve. No such hard conditions for me! There is only one thing that I ask. This is the season that you Christians call the Christmas, and you have taken up the pagan custom of exchanging gifts. Well, if I give to you, you must give to me. It is a small thing, and really the thing you can best afford to part with: a single word—the name of Him you profess to worship. Let me take that word and all that belongs to it entirely out of your life, so that you shall never hear it or speak it again. You will be richer without it. I promise you everything, and this is all I ask in return. Do you consent?"

"Yes. I consent," said Hermas, mocking. "If you can take your price, a word, you can keep your promise, a dream."

The stranger laid the long, cool, wet leaf softly across the young man's eyes. An icicle of pain darted through them; every nerve in his body was drawn together there in a knot of agony.

Then all the tangle of pain seemed to be lifted out of him. A cool languor of delight flowed back through every vein, and he sank into a profound sleep.

III

THERE is a slumber so deep that it annihilates
time. It is like a fragment of eternity. Beneath its
enchantment of vacancy, a day seems like a thousand years, and a thousand years might well pass
as one day.

It was such a sleep that fell upon Hermas in
the Grove of Daphne. An immeasurable period,
an interval of life so blank and empty that he
could not tell whether it was long or short, had
passed over him when his senses began to stir
again. The setting sun was shooting arrows of
gold under the glossy laurel-leaves. He rose and
stretched his arms, grasping a smooth branch
above him and shaking it, to make sure that he
was alive. Then he hurried back toward Antioch,
treading lightly as if on air.

The ground seemed to spring beneath his feet.
Already his life had changed, he knew not how.
Something that did not belong to him had dropped
away; he had returned to a former state of being.

He felt as if anything might happen to him, and he was ready for anything. He was a new man, yet curiously familiar to himself—as if he had done with playing a tiresome part and returned to his natural state. He was buoyant and free, without a care, a doubt, a fear.

As he drew near to his father's house he saw a confusion of servants in the porch, and the old steward ran down to meet him at the gate.

"Lord, we have been seeking you everywhere. The master is at the point of death, and has sent for you. Since the sixth hour he calls your name continually. Come to him quickly, lord, for I fear the time is short."

Hermas entered the house at once; nothing could amaze him to-day. His father lay on an ivory couch in the inmost chamber, with shrunken face and restless eyes, his lean fingers picking incessantly at the silken coverlet.

"My son!" he murmured; "Hermas, my son! It is good that you have come back to me. I have missed you. I was wrong to send you away. You shall never leave me again. You are my son, my heir. I have changed everything. Hermas, my son, come nearer—close beside me. Take my hand, my son!"

The young man obeyed, and, kneeling by the couch, gathered his father's cold, twitching fingers in his firm, warm grasp.

"Hermas, life is passing—long, rich, prosperous; the last sands, I cannot stay them. My religion, a good policy—Julian was my friend. But now he is gone—where? My soul is empty—nothing beyond—very dark—I am afraid. But you know something better. You found something that made you willing to give up your life for it—it must have been almost like dying—yet you were happy. What was it you found? See, I am giving you everything. I have forgiven you. Now forgive me. Tell me, what is it? Your secret, your faith—give it to me before I go."

At the sound of this broken pleading a strange passion of pity and love took the young man by the throat. His voice shook a little as he answered eagerly:

"Father, there is nothing to forgive. I am your

231

son; I will gladly tell you all that I know. I will give you the secret. Father, you must believe with all your heart, and soul, and strength in—"

Where was the word—the word that he had been used to utter night and morning, the word that had meant to him more than he had ever known? What had become of it?

He groped for it in the dark room of his mind. He had thought he could lay his hand upon it in a moment, but it was gone. Some one had taken it away. Everything else was most clear to him: the terror of death; the lonely soul appealing from his father's eyes; the instant need of comfort and help. But at the one point where he looked for help he could find nothing; only an empty space. The word of hope had vanished. He felt for it blindly and in desperate haste.

"Father, wait! I have forgotten something— it has slipped away from me. I shall find it in a moment. There is hope—I will tell you presently —oh, wait!"

The bony hand gripped his like a vice; the

glazed eyes opened wider. "Tell me," whispered the old man; "tell me quickly, for I must go."

The voice sank into a dull rattle. The fingers closed once more, and relaxed. The light behind the eyes went out.

Hermas, the master of the House of the Golden Pillars, was keeping watch by the dead.

IV

THE break with the old life was as clean as if it had been cut with a knife. Some faint image of a hermit's cell, a bare lodging in a back street of Antioch, a class-room full of earnest students, remained in Hermas' memory. Some dull echo of the voice of John the Presbyter, and the measured sound of chanting, and the murmur of great congregations, still lingered in his ears; but it was like something that had happened to another person, something that he had read long ago, but of which he had lost the meaning.

His new life was full and smooth and rich—too rich for any sense of loss to make itself felt. There were a hundred affairs to busy him, and the days ran swiftly by as if they were shod with winged sandals.

Nothing needed to be considered, prepared for, begun. Everything was ready and waiting for him. All that he had to do was to go on.

The estate of Demetrius was even greater than the world had supposed. There were fertile lands in Syria which the emperor had given him, marble-quarries in Phrygia, and forests of valuable timber in Cilicia; the vaults of the villa contained chests of gold and silver; the secret cabinets in the master's room were full of precious stones. The stewards were diligent and faithful. The servants of the household rejoiced at the young master's return. His table was spread; the rose-garland of pleasure was woven for his head; his cup was overflowing with the spicy wine of power.

The period of mourning for his father came at a fortunate moment to seclude and safeguard him from the storm of political troubles and persecutions that fell upon Antioch after the insults offered by the people to the imperial statues in the year 387. The friends of Demetrius, prudent and conservative persons, gathered around Hermas and made him welcome to their circle. Chief among them was Libanius, the sophist, his nearest neighbour, whose daughter Athenaïs had been the playmate of Hermas in the old days.

He had left her a child. He found her a beautiful woman. What transformation is so magical, so charming, as this? To see the uncertain lines of youth rounded into firmness and symmetry, to discover the half-ripe, merry, changing face of the girl matured into perfect loveliness, and looking at you with calm, clear, serious eyes, not forgetting the past, but fully conscious of the changed present—this is to behold a miracle in the flesh.

"Where have you been, these two years?" said Athenaïs, as they walked together through the garden of lilies where they had so often played.

"In a land of tiresome dreams," answered Hermas; "but you have wakened me, and I am never going back again."

It was not to be supposed that the sudden disappearance of Hermas from among his former associates could long remain unnoticed. At first it was a mystery. There was a fear, for two or three days, that he might be lost. Some of his more intimate companions maintained that his devotion had led him out into the desert to join the anchorites. But the news of his return to the House of the Golden Pillars, and of his new life as its master, filtered quickly through the gossip of the city.

Then the church was filled with dismay and grief and reproach. Messengers and letters were sent to Hermas. They disturbed him a little, but they took no hold upon him. It seemed to him as if the messengers spoke in a strange language. As he read the letters there were words blotted out of the writing which made the full sense unintelligible.

His old companions came to reprove him for leaving them, to warn him of the peril of apostasy, to entreat him to return. It all sounded vague and futile. They spoke as if he had betrayed or offended some one; but when they came to name the object of his fear—the one whom he had dis-

pleased, and to whom he should return—he heard
nothing; there was a blur of silence in their speech.
The clock pointed to the hour, but the bell did not
strike. At last Hermas refused to see them any
more.

One day John the Presbyter stood in the atrium.
Hermas was entertaining Libanius and Athenaïs in
the banquet-hall. When the visit of the Presbyter
was announced, the young master loosed a collar
of gold and jewels from his neck, and gave it to
his scribe.

"Take this to John of Antioch, and tell him it
is a gift from his former pupil—as a token of remembrance, or to spend for the poor of the city.
I will always send him what he wants, but it is idle
for us to talk together any more. I do not understand what he says. I have not gone to the temple,
nor offered sacrifice, nor denied his teaching. I
have simply forgotten. I do not think about those
things any longer. I am only living. A happy man
wishes him all happiness and farewell."

But John let the golden collar fall on the marble floor. "Tell your master that we shall talk to-

THE BLUE FLOWER

gether again, in due time," said he, as he passed sadly out of the hall.

The love of Athenaïs and Hermas was like a tiny rivulet that sinks out of sight in a cavern, but emerges again a bright and brimming stream. The careless comradery of childhood was mysteriously changed into a complete companionship.

When Athenaïs entered the House of the Golden Pillars as a bride, all the music of life came with her. Hermas called the feast of her welcome "the banquet of the full chord." Day after day, night after night, week after week, month after month, the bliss of the home unfolded like a rose of a thousand leaves. When a child came to them, a strong, beautiful boy, worthy to be the heir of such a house, the heart of the rose was filled with overflowing fragrance. Happiness was heaped upon happiness. Every wish brought its own accomplishment. Wealth, honour, beauty, peace, love —it was an abundance of felicity so great that the soul of Hermas could hardly contain it.

Strangely enough, it began to press upon him, to trouble him with the very excess of joy. He

238

Take this to John of Antioch and tell him it is a gift from his former pupil.

felt as if there were something yet needed to complete and secure it all. There was an urgency within him, a longing to find some outlet for his feelings, he knew not how—some expression and culmination of his happiness, he knew not what.

Under his joyous demeanour a secret fire of restlessness began to burn—an expectancy of something yet to come which should put the touch of perfection on his life. He spoke of it to Athenaïs, as they sat together, one summer evening, in a bower of jasmine, with their boy playing at their feet. There had been music in the garden; but now the singers and lute-players had withdrawn, leaving the master and mistress alone in the lingering twilight, tremulous with inarticulate melody of unseen birds. There was a secret voice in the hour seeking vainly for utterance—a word waiting to be spoken.

"How deep is our happiness, my beloved!" said Hermas; "deeper than the sea that slumbers yonder, below the city. And yet it is not quite full and perfect. There is a depth of joy that we have not yet known—a repose of happiness that is still beyond us. What is it? I have no superstitions, like the king who cast his signet-ring into the sea because he dreaded that some secret vengeance would fall on his unbroken good fortune. That was an idle terror. But there is something that oppresses me like an invisible burden. There is something still undone, unspoken, unfelt—something that we need to complete everything. Have you not felt it, too? Can you not lead me to it?"

"Yes," she answered, lifting her eyes to his face; "I, too, have felt it, Hermas, this burden, this need, this unsatisfied longing. I think I know what it means. It is gratitude—the language of the heart, the music of happiness. There is no perfect joy without gratitude. But we have never learned it, and the want of it troubles us. It is like being dumb with a heart full of love. We must find the word for it, and say it together. Then we shall be perfectly joined in perfect joy. Come, my dear lord, let us take the boy with us, and give thanks."

Hermas lifted the child in his arms, and turned with Athenaïs into the depth of the garden. There was a dismantled shrine of some forgotten fashion of worship half-hidden among the luxuriant flowers. A fallen image lay beside it, face downward in the grass. They stood there, hand in hand, the boy drowsily resting on his father's shoulder.

Silently the roseate light caressed the tall spires of the cypress-trees; silently the shadows gathered at their feet; silently the tranquil stars looked out from the deepening arch of heaven. The very breath of being paused. It was the hour of culmination, the supreme moment of felicity waiting for its crown. The tones of Hermas were clear and low as he began, half-speaking and half-chanting, in the rhythm of an ancient song:

"Fair is the world, the sea, the sky, the double kingdom of day and night, in the glow of morning, in the shadow of evening, and under the dripping light of stars.

"Fairer still is life in our breasts, with its manifold music and meaning, with its wonder of seeing and hearing and feeling and knowing and being.

"Fairer and still more fair is love, that draws us together, mingles our lives in its flow, and bears them along like a river, strong and clear and swift, reflecting the stars in its bosom.

"Wide is our world; we are rich; we have all things. Life is abundant within us—a measureless deep. Deepest of all is our love, and it longs to speak.

"Come, thou final word; Come, thou crown of speech! Come, thou charm of peace! Open the gates of our hearts. Lift the weight of our joy and bear it upward.

"For all good gifts, for all perfect gifts, for love, for life, for the world, we praise, we bless, we thank—"

As a soaring bird, struck by an arrow, falls headlong from the sky, so the song of Hermas fell. At the end of his flight of gratitude there was nothing—a blank, a hollow space.

He looked for a face, and saw a void. He sought for a hand, and clasped vacancy. His heart was throbbing and swelling with passion; the bell swung to and fro within him, beating from side to side as if it would burst; but not a single note came from it. All the fulness of his feeling, that had risen upward like a fountain, fell back from the empty sky, as cold as snow, as hard as hail, frozen and dead. There was no meaning in his happiness. No one had sent it to him. There was no one to thank for it. His felicity was a closed circle, a wall of ice.

"Let us go back," he said sadly to Athenaïs; "the child is heavy upon my shoulder. We will lay him to sleep, and go into the library. The air grows chilly. We were mistaken. The gratitude of life is only a dream. There is no one to thank."

And in the garden it was already night.

V

No outward change came to the House of the Golden Pillars. Everything moved as smoothly, as delicately, as prosperously, as before. But inwardly there was a subtle, inexplicable transformation. A vague discontent, a final and inevitable sense of incompleteness, overshadowed existence from that night when Hermas realised that his joy could never go beyond itself.

The next morning the old man whom he had seen in the Grove of Daphne, but never since, appeared mysteriously at the door of the house, as if he had been sent for, and entered like an invited guest.

Hermas could not but make him welcome, and at first he tried to regard him with reverence and affection as the one through whom fortune had come. But it was impossible. There was a chill in the inscrutable smile of Marcion, as he called himself, that seemed to mock at reverence. He was in the house as one watching a strange experiment— tranquil, interested, ready to supply anything that might be needed for its completion, but thoroughly indifferent to the feelings of the subject; an anatomist of life, looking curiously to see how long it would continue, and how it would act, after the heart had been removed.

In his presence Hermas was conscious of a certain irritation, a resentful anger against the calm, frigid scrutiny of the eyes that followed him everywhere, like a pair of spies, peering out over the smiling mouth and the long white beard.

THE LOST WORD

"Why do you look at me so curiously?" asked Hermas, one morning, as they sat together in the library. "Do you see anything strange in me?"

"No," answered Marcion; "something familiar."

"And what is that?"

"A singular likeness to a discontented young man that I met some years ago in the Grove of Daphne."

"But why should that interest you? Surely it was to be expected."

"A thing that we expect often surprises us when we see it. Besides, my curiosity is piqued. I suspect you of keeping a secret from me."

"You are jesting with me. There is nothing in my life that you do not know. What is the secret?"

"Nothing more than the wish to have one. You are growing tired of your bargain. The play wearies you. That is foolish. Do you want to try a new part?"

The question was like a mirror upon which one comes suddenly in a half-lighted room. A quick

illumination falls on it, and the passer-by is startled by the look of his own face.

"You are right," said Hermas. "I am tired. We
have been going on stupidly in this house, as if
nothing were possible but what my father had
done before me. There is nothing original in being rich, and well-fed, and well-dressed. Thousands of men have tried it, and have not been satisfied. Let us do something new. Let us make a
mark in the world."

"It is well said," nodded the old man; "you are
speaking again like a man after my own heart.
There is no folly but the loss of an opportunity to
enjoy a new sensation."

From that day Hermas seemed to be possessed
with a perpetual haste, an uneasiness that left him
no repose. The summit of life had been attained,
the highest possible point of felicity. Hencefor-
ward the course could only be at a level—perhaps
downward. It might be brief; at the best it could
not be very long. It was madness to lose a day, an
hour. That would be the only fatal mistake: to
forfeit anything of the bargain that he had made.

He would have it, and hold it, and enjoy it all to the full. The world might have nothing better to give than it had already given; but surely it had many things that were new, and Marcion should help him to find them.

Under his learned counsel the House of the Golden Pillars took on a new magnificence. Artists were brought from Corinth and Rome and Alexandria to adorn it with splendour. Its fame glittered around the world. Banquets of incredible luxury drew the most celebrated guests into its triclinium, and filled them with envious admiration. The bees swarmed and buzzed about the golden hive. The human insects, gorgeous moths of pleasure and greedy flies of appetite, parasites and flatterers and crowds of inquisitive idlers, danced and fluttered in the dazzling light that surrounded Hermas.

Everything that he touched prospered. He bought a tract of land in the Caucasus, and emeralds were discovered among the mountains. He sent a fleet of wheat-ships to Italy, and the price of grain doubled while it was on the way. He sought political favour with the emperor, and was rewarded with the governorship of the city. His name was a word to conjure with.

The beauty of Athenaïs lost nothing with the passing seasons, but grew more perfect, even under the inexplicable shade of dissatisfaction that sometimes veiled it. "Fair as the wife of Hermas" was a proverb in Antioch; and soon men began to add to it, "Beautiful as the son of Hermas"; for the child developed swiftly in that favouring clime. At nine years of age he was straight and strong, firm of limb and clear of eye. His brown head was on a level with his father's heart. He was the jewel of the House of the Golden Pillars; the pride of Hermas, the new Fortunatus.

That year another drop of success fell into his brimming cup. His black Numidian horses, which he had been training for the world-renowned chariot-races of Antioch, won the victory over a score of rivals. Hermas received the prize carelessly from the judge's hands, and turned to drive once more around the circus, to show himself to the people. He lifted the eager boy into the chariot beside him to share his triumph.

Here, indeed, was the glory of his life—this matchless son, his brighter counterpart carved in breathing ivory, touching his arm, and balancing himself proudly on the swaying floor of the chariot. As the horses pranced around the ring, a great shout of applause filled the amphitheatre, and thousands of spectators waved their salutations of praise: "Hail, fortunate Hermas, master of success! Hail, little Hermas, prince of good luck!"

The sudden tempest of acclamation, the swift fluttering of innumerable garments in the air, startled the horses. They dashed violently forward, and plunged upon the bits. The left rein broke. They swerved to the right, swinging the chariot sideways with a grating noise, and dashing it against the stone parapet of the arena. In an instant the wheel was shattered. The axle struck the ground, and the chariot was dragged onward, rocking and staggering.

By a strenuous effort Hermas kept his place on the frail platform, clinging to the unbroken rein. But the boy was tossed lightly from his side at the first shock. His head struck the wall. And when Hermas turned to look for him, he was lying like a broken flower on the sand.

VI

THEY carried the boy in a litter to the House of the Golden Pillars, summoning the most skilful physician of Antioch to attend him. For hours the child was as quiet as death. Hermas watched the white eyelids, folded close like lily-buds at night, even as one watches for the morning. At last they opened; but the fire of fever was burning in the eyes, and the lips were moving in a wild delirium.

Hour after hour that sweet childish voice rang through the halls and chambers of the splendid, helpless house, now rising in shrill calls of distress and senseless laughter, now sinking in weariness and dull moaning. The stars shone and faded; the sun rose and set; the roses bloomed and fell in the garden; the birds sang and slept among the jasmine-bowers. But in the heart of Hermas there was no song, no bloom, no light—only speechless an-

guish, and a certain fearful looking-for of desolation.

He was like a man in a nightmare. He saw the
shapeless terror that was moving toward him, but
he was impotent to stay or to escape it. He had
done all that he could. There was nothing left but
to wait.

He paced to and fro, now hurrying to the boy's
bed as if he could not bear to be away from it,
now turning back as if he could not endure to be
near it. The people of the house, even Athenaïs,
feared to speak to him, there was something so
vacant and desperate in his face.

At nightfall on the second of those eternal days
he shut himself in the library. The unfilled lamp
had gone out, leaving a trail of smoke in the air.
The sprigs of mignonette and rosemary, with
which the room was sprinkled every day, were un-
renewed, and scented the gloom with close odours
of decay. A costly manuscript of Theocritus was
tumbled in disorder on the floor. Hermas sank into
a chair like a man in whom the very spring of being is broken. Through the darkness some one

drew near. He did not even lift his head. A hand touched him; a soft arm was laid over his shoulders. It was Athenaïs, kneeling beside him and speaking very low:

"Hermas—it is almost over—the child! His voice grows weaker hour by hour. He moans and calls for some one to help him; then he laughs. It breaks my heart. He has just fallen asleep. The moon is rising now. Unless a change comes he cannot last till sunrise. Is there nothing we can do? Is there no power that can save him? Is there no one to pity us and spare us? Let us call, let us beg for compassion and help; let us pray for his life!"

Yes; this was what he wanted—this was the only thing that could bring relief: to pray; to pour out his sorrow somewhere; to find a greater strength than his own and cling to it and plead for mercy and help. To leave this undone was to be false to his manhood; it was to be no better than the dumb beasts when their young perish. How could he let his boy suffer and die, without an effort, a cry, a prayer?

He sank on his knees beside Athenaïs.

"Out of the depths—out of the depths we call for pity. The light of our eyes is fading—the child is dying. Oh, the child, the child! Spare the child's life, thou merciful—"

Not a word; only that deathly blank. The hands of Hermas, stretched out in supplication, touched the marble table. He felt the cool hardness of the polished stone beneath his fingers. A roll of papyrus, dislodged by his touch, fell rustling to the floor. Through the open door, faint and far off, came the footsteps of the servants, moving cautiously. The heart of Hermas was like a lump of ice in his bosom. He rose slowly to his feet, lifting Athenaïs with him.

"It is in vain," he said; "there is nothing for us to do. Long ago I knew something. I think it would have helped us. But I have forgotten it. It is all gone. But I would give all that I have, if I could bring it back again now, at this hour, in this time of our bitter trouble."

A slave entered the room while he was speaking, and approached hesitatingly.

"Master," he said, "John of Antioch, whom we were forbidden to admit to the house, has come again. He would take no denial. Even now he waits in the peristyle; and the old man Marcion is with him, seeking to turn him away."

"Come," said Hermas to his wife, "let us go to him."

In the central hall the two men were standing; Marcion, with disdainful eyes and sneering lips, taunting the unbidden guest; John, silent, quiet, patient, while the wondering slaves looked on in dismay. He lifted his searching gaze to the haggard face of Hermas.

"My son, I knew that I should see you again, even though you did not send for me. I have come to you because I have heard that you are in trouble."

"It is true," answered Hermas, passionately; "we are in trouble, desperate trouble, trouble accursed. Our child is dying. We are poor, we are destitute, we are afflicted. In all this house, in all the world, there is no one that can help us. I knew something long ago, when I was with you,—a

254

word, a name,—in which we might have found hope. But I have lost it. I gave it to this man. He has taken it away from me forever."

He pointed to Marcion. The old man's lips curled scornfully. "A word, a name!" he sneered. "What is that, O most wise man and holy Presbyter? A thing of air, a thing that men make to describe their own dreams and fancies. Who would go about to rob any one of such a thing as that? It is a prize that only a fool would think of taking. Besides, the young man parted with it of his own free will. He bargained with me cleverly. I promised him wealth and pleasure and fame. What did he give in return? An empty name, which was a burden—"

"Servant of demons, be still!" The voice of John rang clear, like a trumpet, through the hall. "There is a name which none shall dare to take in vain. There is a name which none can lose without being lost. There is a name at which the devils tremble. Go quickly, before I speak it!"

Marcion shrank into the shadow of one of the pillars. A lamp near him tottered on its pedestal and fell with a crash. In the confusion he vanished, as noiselessly as a shade.

John turned to Hermas, and his tone softened as he said: "My son, you have sinned deeper than you know. The word with which you parted so lightly is the keyword of all life. Without it the world has no meaning, existence no peace, death no refuge. It is the word that purifies love, and comforts grief, and keeps hope alive forever. It is the most precious word that ever ear has heard, or mind has known, or heart has conceived. It is the name of Him who has given us life and breath and all things richly to enjoy; the name of Him who, though we may forget Him, never forgets us; the name of Him who pities us as you pity your suffering child; the name of Him who, though we wander far from Him, seeks us in the wilderness, and sent His Son, even as His Son has sent me this night, to breathe again that forgotten name in the heart that is perishing without it. Listen, my son, listen with all your soul to the blessed name of God our Father."

The cold agony in the breast of Hermas dissolved like a fragment of ice that melts in the summer sea. A sense of sweet release spread through him from head to foot. The lost was found. The dew of peace fell on his parched soul, and the withering flower of human love raised its head again. He stood upright, and lifted his hands high toward heaven.

"Out of the depths have I cried unto Thee, O Lord! O my God, be merciful to me, for my soul trusteth in Thee. My God, Thou hast given; take not Thy gift away from me, O my God! Spare the life of this my child, O Thou God, my Father, my Father!"

A deep hush followed the cry. "Listen!" whispered Athenaïs, breathlessly.

Was it an echo? It could not be, for it came again—the voice of the child, clear and low, waking from sleep, and calling: "Father!"

THE FIRST CHRISTMAS-TREE

THE FIRST CHRISTMAS-TREE

I

THE day before Christmas, in the year of our Lord 722.

Broad snow-meadows glistening white along the banks of the river Moselle; steep hill-sides blooming with mystic forget-me-not where the glow of the setting sun cast long shadows down their eastern slope; an arch of clearest, deepest gentian bending overhead; in the centre of the aerial garden the walls of the cloister of Pfalzel, steel-blue to the east, violet to the west; silence over all,—a gentle, eager, conscious stillness, diffused through the air, as if earth and sky were hushing themselves to hear the voice of the river faintly murmuring down the valley.

In the cloister, too, there was silence at the sunset hour. All day long there had been a strange and joyful stir among the nuns. A breeze of curiosity and excitement had swept along the corridors and through every quiet cell. A famous visitor had come to the convent.

It was Winfried of England, whose name in the Roman tongue was Boniface, and whom men called the Apostle of Germany. A great preacher; a wonderful scholar; but, more than all, a daring traveller, a venturesome pilgrim, a priest of romance.

He had left his home and his fair estate in Wessex; he would not stay in the rich monastery of Nutescelle, even though they had chosen him as the abbot; he had refused a bishopric at the court of King Karl. Nothing would content him but to go out into the wild woods and preach to the heathen.

Through the forests of Hesse and Thuringia, and along the borders of Saxony, he had wandered for years, with a handful of companions, sleeping under the trees, crossing mountains and marshes, now here, now there, never satisfied with ease and comfort, always in love with hardship and danger.

What a man he was! Fair and slight, but straight as a spear and strong as an oaken staff.

THE FIRST CHRISTMAS-TREE

His face was still young; the smooth skin was bronzed by wind and sun. His gray eyes, clean and kind, flashed like fire when he spoke of his adventures, and of the evil deeds of the false priests with whom he contended.

What tales he had told that day! Not of miracles wrought by sacred relics; not of courts and councils and splendid cathedrals; though he knew much of these things. But to-day he had spoken of long journeyings by sea and land; of perils by fire and flood; of wolves and bears, and fierce snowstorms, and black nights in the lonely forest; of dark altars of heathen gods, and weird, bloody sacrifices, and narrow escapes from murderous bands of wandering savages.

The little novices had gathered around him, and their faces had grown pale and their eyes bright as they listened with parted lips, entranced in admiration, twining their arms about one another's shoulders and holding closely together, half in fear, half in delight. The older nuns had turned from their tasks and paused, in passing by, to hear the pilgrim's story. Too well they knew the truth of what he spoke. Many a one among them had seen the smoke rising from the ruins of her father's roof. Many a one had a brother far away in the wild country to whom her heart went out night and day, wondering if he were still among the living.

But now the excitements of that wonderful day were over; the hour of the evening meal had come; the inmates of the cloister were assembled in the refectory.

On the daïs sat the stately Abbess Addula, daughter of King Dagobert, looking a princess indeed, in her purple tunic, with the hood and cuffs of her long white robe trimmed with ermine, and a snowy veil resting like a crown on her silver hair. At her right hand was the honoured guest, and at her left hand her grandson, the young Prince Gregor, a big, manly boy, just returned from school.

The long, shadowy hall, with its dark-brown rafters and beams; the double row of nuns, with their pure veils and fair faces; the ruddy glow of the slanting sunbeams striking upward through the tops of the windows and painting a pink glow high up on the walls,—it was all as beautiful as a picture, and as silent. For this was the rule of the cloister, that at the table all should sit in stillness for a little while, and then one should read aloud, while the rest listened.

"It is the turn of my grandson to read to-day," said the abbess to Winfried; "we shall see how much he has learned in the school. Read, Gregor; the place in the book is marked."

The lad rose from his seat and turned the pages of the manuscript. It was a copy of Jerome's version of the Scriptures in Latin, and the marked place was in the letter of St. Paul to the Ephesians, —the passage where he describes the preparation of the Christian as a warrior arming for battle. The young voice rang out clearly, rolling the sonorous words, without slip or stumbling, to the end of the chapter.

Winfried listened smiling. "That was bravely read, my son," said he, as the reader paused. "Understandest thou what thou readest?"

"Surely, father," answered the boy; "it was taught me by the masters at Treves; and we have

265

read this epistle from beginning to end, so that I almost know it by heart."

Then he began to repeat the passage, turning away from the page as if to show his skill.

But Winfried stopped him with a friendly lifting of the hand.

"Not so, my son; that was not my meaning. When we pray, we speak to God. When we read, God speaks to us. I ask whether thou hast heard what He has said to thee in the common speech. Come, give us again the message of the warrior and his armour and his battle, in the mother-tongue, so that all can understand it."

The boy hesitated, blushed, stammered; then he came around to Winfried's seat, bringing the book. "Take the book, my father," he cried, "and read it for me. I cannot see the meaning plain, though I love the sound of the words. Religion I know, and the doctrines of our faith, and the life of priests and nuns in the cloister, for which my grandmother designs me, though it likes me little. And fighting I know, and the life of warriors and heroes, for I have read of it in Virgil and the an-

cients, and heard a bit from the soldiers at Treves;
and I would fain taste more of it, for it likes me
much. But how the two lives fit together, or what
need there is of armour for a clerk in holy orders,
I can never see. Tell me the meaning, for if there
is a man in all the world that knows it, I am sure
it is thou."

So Winfried took the book and closed it, clasping the boy's hand with his own.

"Let us first dismiss the others to their vespers,"
said he, "lest they should be weary."

A sign from the abbess; a chanted benediction;
a murmuring of sweet voices and a soft rustling of
many feet over the rushes on the floor; the gentle
tide of noise flowed out through the doors and
ebbed away down the corridors; the three at the
head of the table were left alone in the darkening
room.

Then Winfried began to translate the parable
of the soldier into the realities of life.

At every turn he knew how to flash a new
light into the picture out of his own experience.
He spoke of the combat with self, and of the

wrestling with dark spirits in solitude. He spoke of the demons that men had worshipped for centuries in the wilderness, and whose malice they invoked against the stranger who ventured into the gloomy forest. Gods, they called them, and told weird tales of their dwelling among the impenetrable branches of the oldest trees and in the caverns of the shaggy hills; of their riding on the wind-horses and hurling spears of lightning against their foes. Gods they were not, but foul spirits of the air, rulers of the darkness. Was there not glory and honour in fighting them, in daring their anger under the shield of faith, in putting them to flight with the sword of truth? What better adventure could a brave man ask than to go forth against them, and wrestle with them, and conquer them?

"Look you, my friends," said Winfried, "how sweet and peaceful is this convent to-night! It is a garden full of flowers in the heart of winter; a nest among the branches of a great tree shaken by the winds; a still haven on the edge of a tempestuous sea. And this is what religion means for those who are chosen and called to quietude and prayer and meditation.

"But out yonder in the wide forest, who knows what storms are raving to-night in the hearts of men, though all the woods are still? who knows what haunts of wrath and cruelty are closed to-night against the advent of the Prince of Peace? And shall I tell you what religion means to those who are called and chosen to dare, and to fight, and to conquer the world for Christ? It means to go against the strongholds of the adversary. It means to struggle to win an entrance for the Master everywhere. What helmet is strong enough for this strife save the helmet of salvation? What breastplate can guard a man against these fiery darts but the breastplate of righteousness? What shoes can stand the wear of these journeys but the preparation of the gospel of peace?"

"Shoes?" he cried again, and laughed as if a sudden thought had struck him. He thrust out his foot, covered with a heavy cowhide boot, laced high about his leg with thongs of skin.

"Look here,—how a fighting man of the cross is

shod! I have seen the boots of the Bishop of Tours, —white kid, broidered with silk; a day in the bogs would tear them to shreds. I have seen the sandals that the monks use on the highroads,—yes, and worn them; ten pair of them have I worn out and thrown away in a single journey. Now I shoe my feet with the toughest hides, hard as iron; no rock can cut them, no branches can tear them. Yet more than one pair of these have I outworn, and many more shall I outwear ere my journeys are ended. And I think, if God is gracious to me, that I shall die wearing them. Better so than in a soft bed with silken coverings. The boots of a warrior, a hunter, a woodsman,—these are my preparation of the gospel of peace.

"Come, Gregor," he said, laying his brown hand on the youth's shoulder, "come, wear the forester's boots with me. This is the life to which we are called. Be strong in the Lord, a hunter of the demons, a subduer of the wilderness, a woodsman of the faith. Come."

The boy's eyes sparkled. He turned to his grandmother. She shook her head vigorously.

"Nay, father," she said, "draw not the lad away from my side with these wild words. I need him to help me with my labours, to cheer my old age."

"Do you need him more than the Master does?" asked Winfried; "and will you take the wood that is fit for a bow to make a distaff?"

"But I fear for the child. Thy life is too hard for him. He will perish with hunger in the woods."

"Once," said Winfried, smiling, "we were camped on the bank of the river Ohru. The table was set for the morning meal, but my comrades cried that it was empty; the provisions were exhausted; we must go without breakfast, and perhaps starve before we could escape from the wilderness. While they complained, a fish-hawk flew up from the river with flapping wings, and let fall a great pike in the midst of the camp. There was food enough and to spare! Never have I seen the righteous forsaken, nor his seed begging bread."

"But the fierce pagans of the forest," cried the abbess,—"they may pierce the boy with their arrows, or dash out his brains with their axes. He is but a child, too young for the danger and the strife."

"A child in years," replied Winfried, "but a man in spirit. And if the hero fall early in the battle, he wears the brighter crown, not a leaf withered, not a flower fallen."

The aged princess trembled a little. She drew Gregor close to her side, and laid her hand gently on his brown hair.

"I am not sure that he wants to leave me yet. Besides, there is no horse in the stable to give him, now, and he cannot go as befits the grandson of a king."

Gregor looked straight into her eyes.

"Grandmother," said he, "dear grandmother, if thou wilt not give me a horse to ride with this man of God, I will go with him afoot."

II

Two years had passed since that Christmas-eve in the cloister of Pfalzel. A little company of pilgrims, less than a score of men, were travelling slowly northward through the wide forest that rolled over the hills of central Germany.

At the head of the band marched Winfried, clad in a tunic of fur, with his long black robe girt high above his waist, so that it might not hinder his stride. His hunter's boots were crusted with snow. Drops of ice sparkled like jewels along the thongs that bound his legs. There were no other ornaments of his dress except the bishop's cross hanging on his breast, and the silver clasp that fastened his cloak about his neck. He carried a strong, tall staff in his hand, fashioned at the top into the form of a cross.

Close beside him, keeping step like a familiar comrade, was the young Prince Gregor. Long marches through the wilderness had stretched his legs and broadened his back, and made a man of him in stature as well as in spirit. His jacket and cap were of wolf-skin, and on his shoulder he carried an axe, with broad, shining blade. He was a mighty woodsman now, and could make a spray of chips fly around him as he hewed his way through the trunk of a pine-tree.

Behind these leaders followed a pair of teamsters, guiding a rude sledge, loaded with food and the equipage of the camp, and drawn by two big, shaggy horses, blowing thick clouds of steam from their frosty nostrils. Tiny icicles hung from the hairs on their lips. Their flanks were smoking. They sank above the fetlocks at every step in the soft snow.

Last of all came the rear guard, armed with bows and javelins. It was no child's play, in those days, to cross Europe afoot.

The weird woodland, sombre and illimitable, covered hill and vale, table-land and mountain-peak. There were wide moors where the wolves hunted in packs as if the devil drove them, and tangled thickets where the lynx and the boar made their lairs. Fierce bears lurked among the rocky passes, and had not yet learned to fear the face of man. The gloomy recesses of the forest gave shelter to inhabitants who were still more cruel and dangerous than beasts of prey,—outlaws and sturdy robbers and mad were-wolves and bands of wandering pillagers.

THE FIRST CHRISTMAS-TREE

The pilgrim who would pass from the mouth of the Tiber to the mouth of the Rhine must trust in God and keep his arrows loose in the quiver.

The travellers were surrounded by an ocean of trees, so vast, so full of endless billows, that it seemed to be pressing on every side to overwhelm them. Gnarled oaks, with branches twisted and knotted as if in rage, rose in groves like tidal waves. Smooth forests of beech-trees, round and gray, swept over the knolls and slopes of land in a mighty ground-swell. But most of all, the multitude of pines and firs, innumerable and monotonous, with straight, stark trunks, and branches woven together in an unbroken flood of darkest green, crowded through the valleys and over the hills, rising on the highest ridges into ragged crests, like the foaming edge of breakers.

Through this sea of shadows ran a narrow stream of shining whiteness,—an ancient Roman road, covered with snow. It was as if some great ship had ploughed through the green ocean long ago, and left behind it a thick, smooth wake of foam. Along this open track the travellers held their way,—heavily, for the drifts were deep; warily, for the hard winter had driven many packs of wolves down from the moors.

The steps of the pilgrims were noiseless; but the sledges creaked over the dry snow, and the panting of the horses throbbed through the still air. The pale-blue shadows on the western side of the road grew longer. The sun, declining through its shallow arch, dropped behind the tree-tops. Darkness followed swiftly, as if it had been a bird of prey waiting for this sign to swoop down upon the world.

"Father," said Gregor to the leader, "surely this day's march is done. It is time to rest, and eat, and sleep. If we press onward now, we cannot see our steps; and will not that be against the word of the psalmist David, who bids us not to put confidence in the legs of a man?"

Winfried laughed. "Nay, my son Gregor," said he, "thou hast tripped, even now, upon thy text. For David said only, 'I take no pleasure in the legs of a man.' And so say I, for I am not minded to spare thy legs or mine, until we come farther on our way, and do what must be done this night. Draw thy belt tighter, my son, and hew me out this tree that is fallen across the road, for our camp-ground is not here."

The youth obeyed; two of the foresters sprang to help him; and while the soft fir-wood yielded to the stroke of the axes, and the snow flew from the bending branches, Winfried turned and spoke to his followers in a cheerful voice, that refreshed them like wine.

"Courage, brothers, and forward yet a little! The moon will light us presently, and the path is plain. Well know I that the journey is weary; and my own heart wearies also for the home in England, where those I love are keeping feast this Christmas-eve. But we have work to do before we feast to-night. For this is the Yuletide, and the heathen people of the forest are gathered at the thunder-oak of Geismar to worship their god, Thor. Strange things will be seen there, and deeds which make the soul black. But we are sent to lighten their darkness; and we will teach our kinsmen to keep a Christmas with us such as the woodland has never known. Forward, then, and stiffen up the feeble knees!"

A murmur of assent came from the men. Even the horses seemed to take fresh heart. They flattened their backs to draw the heavy loads, and blew the frost from their nostrils as they pushed ahead.

The night grew broader and less oppressive. A gate of brightness was opened secretly somewhere in the sky. Higher and higher swelled the clear moon-flood, until it poured over the eastern wall of forest into the road. A drove of wolves howled faintly in the distance, but they were receding, and the sound soon died away. The stars sparkled merrily through the stringent air; the small, round moon shone like silver; little breaths of dreaming wind wandered across the pointed fir-tops, as the pilgrims toiled bravely onward, following their clew of light through a labyrinth of darkness.

After a while the road began to open out a little. There were spaces of meadow-land, fringed with alders, behind which a boisterous river ran clashing through spears of ice.

Rude houses of hewn logs appeared in the open-

The fields around lay bare to the moon.

ings, each one casting a patch of inky shadow upon the snow. Then the travellers passed a larger group of dwellings, all silent and unlighted; and beyond, they saw a great house, with many outbuildings and inclosed courtyards, from which the hounds bayed furiously, and a noise of stamping horses came from the stalls. But there was no other sound of life. The fields around lay naked to the moon. They saw no man, except that once, on a path that skirted the farther edge of a meadow, three dark figures passed them, running very swiftly.

Then the road plunged again into a dense thicket, traversed it, and climbing to the left, emerged suddenly upon a glade, round and level except at the northern side, where a hillock was crowned with a huge oak-tree. It towered above the heath, a giant with contorted arms, beckoning to the host of lesser trees. "Here," cried Winfried, as his eyes flashed and his hand lifted his heavy staff, "here is the Thunder-oak; and here the cross of Christ shall break the hammer of the false god Thor."

III

WITHERED leaves still clung to the branches of the oak: torn and faded banners of the departed summer. The bright crimson of autumn had long since disappeared, bleached away by the storms and the cold. But to-night these tattered remnants of glory were red again: ancient bloodstains against the dark-blue sky. For an immense fire had been kindled in front of the tree. Tongues of ruddy flame, fountains of ruby sparks, ascended through the spreading limbs and flung a fierce illumination upward and around. The pale, pure moonlight that bathed the surrounding forests was quenched and eclipsed here. Not a beam of it sifted through the branches of the oak. It stood like a pillar of cloud between the still light of heaven and the crackling, flashing fire of earth.

But the fire itself was invisible to Winfried and his companions. A great throng of people were gathered around it in a half-circle, their backs to the open glade, their faces toward the oak. Seen against that glowing background, it was but the silhouette of a crowd, vague, black, formless, mysterious.

The travellers paused for a moment at the edge of the thicket, and took counsel together.

"It is the assembly of the tribe," said one of the foresters, "the great night of the council. I heard of it three days ago, as we passed through one of the villages. All who swear by the old gods have been summoned. They will sacrifice a steed to the god of war, and drink blood, and eat horse-flesh to make them strong. It will be at the peril of our lives if we approach them. At least we must hide the cross, if we would escape death."

"Hide me no cross," cried Winfried, lifting his staff, "for I have come to show it, and to make these blind folk see its power. There is more to be done here to-night than the slaying of a steed, and a greater evil to be stayed than the shameful eating of meat sacrificed to idols. I have seen it in a dream. Here the cross must stand and be our rede."

At his command the sledge was left in the border

of the wood, with two of the men to guard it, and the rest of the company moved forward across the open ground. They approached unnoticed, for all the multitude were looking intently toward the fire at the foot of the oak.

Then Winfried's voice rang out, "Hail, ye sons of the forest! A stranger claims the warmth of your fire in the winter night."

Swiftly, and as with a single motion, a thousand eyes were bent upon the speaker. The semi-circle opened silently in the middle; Winfried entered with his followers; it closed again behind them.

Then, as they looked round the curving ranks, they saw that the hue of the assemblage was not black, but white, — dazzling, radiant, solemn. White, the robes of the women clustered together at the points of the wide crescent; white, the glittering byrnies of the warriors standing in close ranks; white, the fur mantles of the aged men who held the central palace in the circle; white, with the shimmer of silver ornaments and the purity of lamb's-wool, the raiment of a little group of children who stood close by the fire; white, with awe and fear, the faces of all who looked at them; and over all the flickering, dancing radiance of the flames played and glimmered like a faint, vanishing tinge of blood on snow.

The only figure untouched by the glow was the old priest, Hunrad, with his long, spectral robe, flowing hair and beard, and dead-pale face, who stood with his back to the fire and advanced slowly to meet the strangers.

"Who are you? Whence come you, and what seek you here?"

"Your kinsman am I, of the German brotherhood," answered Winfried, "and from England, beyond the sea, have I come to bring you a greeting from that land, and a message from the All-Father, whose servant I am."

"Welcome, then," said Hunrad, "welcome, kinsman, and be silent; for what passes here is too high to wait, and must be done before the moon crosses the middle heaven, unless, indeed, thou hast some sign or token from the gods. Canst thou work miracles?"

THE BLUE FLOWER

The question came sharply, as if a sudden gleam of hope had flashed through the tangle of the old priest's mind. But Winfried's voice sank lower and a cloud of disappointment passed over his face as he replied: "Nay, miracles have I never wrought, though I have heard of many; but the All-Father has given no power to my hands save such as belongs to common man."

"Stand still, then, thou common man," said Hunrad, scornfully, "and behold what the gods have called us hither to do. This night is the death-night of the sun-god, Baldur the Beautiful, beloved of gods and men. This night is the hour of darkness and the power of winter, of sacrifice and mighty fear. This night the great Thor, the god of thunder and war, to whom this oak is sacred, is grieved for the death of Baldur, and angry with this people because they have forsaken his worship. Long is it since an offering has been laid upon his altar, long since the roots of his holy tree have been fed with blood. Therefore its leaves have withered before the time, and its boughs are heavy with death. Therefore the Slavs

284

and the Wends have beaten us in battle. Therefore the harvests have failed, and the wolf-hordes have ravaged the folds, and the strength has departed from the bow, and the wood of the spear has broken, and the wild boar has slain the huntsman. Therefore the plague has fallen on our dwellings, and the dead are more than the living in all our villages. Answer me, ye people, are not these things true? "

A hoarse sound of approval ran through the circle. A chant, in which the voices of the men and women blended, like the shrill wind in the pine-trees above the rumbling thunder of a waterfall, rose and fell in rude cadences.

> *O Thor, the Thunderer,*
> *Mighty and merciless,*
> *Spare us from smiting!*
> *Heave not thy hammer,*
> *Angry, against us;*
> *Plague not thy people.*
> *Take from our treasure*
> *Richest of ransom.*
> *Silver we send thee,*

Jewels and javelins,
Goodliest garments,
All our possessions,
Priceless, we proffer.
Sheep will we slaughter,
Steeds will we sacrifice;
Bright blood shall bathe thee,
O tree of Thunder,
Life-floods shall lave thee,
Strong wood of wonder.
Mighty, have mercy,
Smite us no more,
Spare us and save us,
Spare us, Thor! Thor!

With two great shouts the song ended, and a stillness followed so intense that the crackling of the fire was heard distinctly. The old priest stood silent for a moment. His shaggy brows swept down over his eyes like ashes quenching flame. Then he lifted his face and spoke.

"None of these things will please the god. More costly is the offering that shall cleanse your sin, more precious the crimson dew that shall send

new life into this holy tree of blood. Thor claims
your dearest and your noblest gift."

Hunrad moved nearer to the group of children who stood watching the fire and the swarms of
spark-serpents darting upward. They had heeded
none of the priest's words, and did not notice now
that he approached them, so eager were they to
see which fiery snake would go highest among the
oak branches. Foremost among them, and most intent on the pretty game, was a boy like a sunbeam, slender and quick, with blithe brown eyes
and laughing lips. The priest's hand was laid upon
his shoulder. The boy turned and looked up in his
face.

"Here," said the old man, with his voice vibrating as when a thick rope is strained by a ship
swinging from her moorings, "here is the chosen
one, the eldest son of the Chief, the darling of the
people. Hearken, Bernhard, wilt thou go to Valhalla, where the heroes dwell with the gods, to bear
a message to Thor?"

The boy answered, swift and clear:

"Yes, priest, I will go if my father bids me. Is

it far away? Shall I run quickly? Must I take my bow and arrows for the wolves?"

The boy's father, the Chieftain Gundhar, standing among his bearded warriors, drew his breath deep, and leaned so heavily on the handle of his spear that the wood cracked. And his wife, Irma, bending forward from the ranks of women, pushed the golden hair from her forehead with one hand. The other dragged at the silver chain about her neck until the rough links pierced her flesh, and the red drops fell unheeded on her breast.

A sigh passed through the crowd, like the murmur of the forest before the storm breaks. Yet no one spoke save Hunrad:

"Yes, my Prince, both bow and spear shalt thou have, for the way is long, and thou art a brave huntsman. But in darkness thou must journey for a little space, and with eyes blindfolded. Fearest thou?"

"Naught fear I," said the boy, "neither darkness, nor the great bear, nor the were-wolf. For I am Gunhar's son, and the defender of my folk."

It poised for an instant above the child's fair head—death cruel and imminent.

Then the priest led the child in his raiment of lamb's-wool to a broad stone in front of the fire. He gave him his little bow tipped with silver, and his spear with shining head of steel. He bound the child's eyes with a white cloth, and bade him kneel beside the stone with his face to the east. Unconsciously the wide arc of spectators drew inward toward the centre, as the ends of the bow draw together when the cord is stretched. Winfried moved noiselessly until he stood close behind the priest.

The old man stooped to lift a black hammer of stone from the ground,—the sacred hammer of the god Thor. Summoning all the strength of his withered arms, he swung it high in the air. It poised for an instant above the child's fair head—then turned to fall.

One keen cry shrilled out from where the women stood: "Me! take me! not Bernhard!"

The flight of the mother toward her child was swift as the falcon's swoop. But swifter still was the hand of the deliverer.

Winfried's heavy staff thrust mightily against

the hammer's handle as it fell. Sideways it glanced from the old man's grasp, and the black stone, striking on the altar's edge, split in twain. A shout of awe and joy rolled along the living circle. The branches of the oak shivered. The flames leaped higher. As the shout died away the people saw the lady Irma, with her arms clasped round her child, and above them, on the altar-stone, Winfried, his face shining like the face of an angel.

IV

A SWIFT mountain-flood rolling down its channel; a huge rock tumbling from the hill-side and falling in mid-stream: the baffled waters broken and confused, pausing in their flow, dash high against the rock, foaming and murmuring, with divided impulse, uncertain whether to turn to the right or the left.

Even so Winfried's bold deed fell into the midst of the thoughts and passions of the council. They were at a standstill. Anger and wonder, reverence and joy and confusion surged through the crowd.

They knew not which way to move: to resent the intrusion of the stranger as an insult to their gods, or to welcome him as the rescuer of their prince.

The old priest crouched by the altar, silent. Conflicting counsels troubled the air. Let the sacrifice go forward; the gods must be appeased. Nay, the boy must not die; bring the chieftain's best horse and slay it in his stead; it will be enough; the holy tree loves the blood of horses. Not so, there is a better counsel yet; seize the stranger whom the gods have led hither as a victim and make his life pay the forfeit of his daring.

The withered leaves on the oak rustled and whispered overhead. The fire flared and sank again. The angry voices clashed against each other and fell like opposing waves. Then the chieftain Gundhar struck the earth with his spear and gave his decision.

"All have spoken, but none are agreed. There is no voice of the council. Keep silence now, and let the stranger speak. His words shall give us judgment, whether he is to live or to die."

Winfried lifted himself high upon the altar, drew a roll of parchment from his bosom, and began to read.

"A letter from the great Bishop of Rome, who sits on a golden throne, to the people of the forest, Hessians and Thuringians, Franks and Saxons. *In nomine Domini, sanctae et individuae Trinitatis, amen!*"

A murmur of awe ran through the crowd. "It is the sacred tongue of the Romans; the tongue that is heard and understood by the wise men of every land. There is magic in it. Listen!"

Winfried went on to read the letter, translating it into the speech of the people.

"We have sent unto you our Brother Boniface, and appointed him your bishop, that he may teach you the only true faith, and baptise you, and lead you back from the ways of error to the path of salvation. Hearken to him in all things like a father. Bow your hearts to his teaching. He comes not for earthly gain, but for the gain of your souls. Depart from evil works. Worship not the false gods, for they are devils. Offer no more bloody sacrifices, nor eat the flesh of horses, but do as our Brother Boniface commands you. Build a house for him that he may dwell among you, and a church where you may offer your prayers to the only living God, the Almighty King of Heaven."

It was a splendid message: proud, strong, peaceful, loving. The dignity of the words imposed mightily upon the hearts of the people. They were quieted as men who have listened to a lofty strain of music.

"Tell us, then," said Gundhar, "what is the word that thou bringest to us from the Almighty? What is thy counsel for the tribes of the woodland on this night of sacrifice?"

"This is the word, and this is the counsel," answered Winfried. "Not a drop of blood shall fall to-night, save that which pity has drawn from the breast of your princess, in love for her child. Not a life shall be blotted out in the darkness to-night; but the great shadow of the tree which hides you from the light of heaven shall be swept away. For this is the birth-night of the white Christ, son of the All-Father, and Saviour of mankind. Fairer is He than Baldur the Beautiful, greater than Odin the Wise, kinder than Freya the Good. Since He has come to earth the bloody sacrifice must cease. The dark Thor, on whom you vainly call, is dead. Deep in the shades of Niffelheim he is lost forever. His power in the world is broken. Will you serve a helpless god? See, my brothers, you call this tree his oak. Does he dwell here? Does he protect it?"

A troubled voice of assent rose from the throng. The people stirred uneasily. Women covered their eyes. Hunrad lifted his head and muttered hoarsely, "Thor! take vengeance! Thor!"

Winfried beckoned to Gregor. "Bring the axes, thine and one for me. Now, young woodsman, show thy craft! The king-tree of the forest must fall, and swiftly, or all is lost!"

The two men took their places facing each other, one on each side of the oak. Their cloaks were flung aside, their heads bare. Carefully they felt the ground with their feet, seeking a firm grip of the earth. Firmly they grasped the axe-helves and swung the shining blades.

"Tree-god!" cried Winfried, "art thou angry? Thus we smite thee!"

"Tree - god!" answered Gregor, "art thou mighty? Thus we fight thee!"

Clang! clang! the alternate strokes beat time upon the hard, ringing wood. The axe-heads glittered in their rhythmic flight, like fierce eagles circling about their quarry.

The broad flakes of wood flew from the deepening gashes in the sides of the oak. The huge trunk quivered. There was a shuddering in the branches. Then the great wonder of Winfried's life came to pass.

Out of the stillness of the winter night, a mighty rushing noise sounded overhead.

Was it the ancient gods on their white battle-steeds, with their black hounds of wrath and their arrows of lightning, sweeping through the air to destroy their foes?

A strong, whirling wind passed over the tree-tops. It gripped the oak by its branches and tore

THE BLUE FLOWER

it from the roots. Backward it fell, like a ruined tower, groaning and crashing as it split asunder in four great pieces.

Winfried let his axe drop, and bowed his head for a moment in the presence of almighty power.

Then he turned to the people, "Here is the timber," he cried, "already felled and split for your new building. On this spot shall rise a chapel to the true God and his servant St. Peter.

"And here," said he, as his eyes fell on a young fir-tree, standing straight and green, with its top pointing toward the stars, amid the divided ruins of the fallen oak, "here is the living tree, with no stain of blood upon it, that shall be the sign of your new worship. See how it points to the sky. Call it the tree of the Christ-child. Take it up and carry it to the chieftain's hall. You shall go no more into the shadows of the forest to keep your feasts with secret rites of shame. You shall keep them at home, with laughter and songs and rites of love. The thunder-oak has fallen, and I think the day is coming when there shall not be a home

296

in all Germany where the children are not gathered around the green fir-tree to rejoice in the birth-night of Christ."

So they took the little fir from its place, and carried it in joyous procession to the edge of the glade, and laid it on the sledge. The horses tossed their heads and drew their load bravely, as if the new burden had made it lighter.

When they came to the house of Gundhar, he bade them throw open the doors of the hall and set the tree in the midst of it. They kindled lights among the branches until it seemed to be tangled full of fire-flies. The children encircled it, wondering, and the sweet odour of the balsam filled the house.

Then Winfried stood beside the chair of Gundhar, on the daïs at the end of the hall, and told the story of Bethlehem; of the babe in the manger, of the shepherds on the hills, of the host of angels and their midnight song. All the people listened, charmed into stillness.

But the boy Bernhard, on Irma's knee, folded in her soft arms, grew restless as the story lengthened, and began to prattle softly at his mother's ear.

"Mother," whispered the child, "why did you cry out so loud, when the priest was going to send me to Valhalla?"

"Oh, hush, my child," answered the mother, and pressed him closer to her side.

"Mother," whispered the boy again, laying his finger on the stains upon her breast, "see, your dress is red! What are these stains? Did some one hurt you?"

The mother closed his mouth with a kiss. "Dear, be still, and listen!"

The boy obeyed. His eyes were heavy with sleep. But he heard the last words of Winfried as he spoke of the angelic messengers, flying over the hills of Judea and singing as they flew. The child wondered and dreamed and listened. Suddenly his face grew bright. He put his lips close to Irma's cheek again.

"Oh, mother!" he whispered very low, "do not speak. Do you hear them? Those angels have come back again. They are singing now behind the tree."

THE FIRST CHRISTMAS-TREE

And some say that it was true; but others say that it was only Gregor and his companions at the lower end of the hall, chanting their Christmas-hymn:

> *All glory be to God on high,*
> *And on the earth be peace!*
> *Good-will, henceforth, from heaven to men*
> *Begin and never cease.*